The *Moonraker* was gone. All that was left of the once-beautiful square-rigger and her eighty-three passengers and crew were eight men, a woman, and a cabin boy.

Just nine days before, the proud ship sailed from Melbourne, Australia, intending to brave the big seas and sail around Cape Horn for Boston. But fate intervened and like a phantom ship sailing a ghostly sea, the square-rigger lay wrapped in a heavy gray mist so thick you could walk on it. Well off course in treacherous waters and without wind or visibility, the *Moonraker* was pushed relentlessly by heavy swells into a monstrous sea cavern, only to be trapped, ripped apart by the pounding sea, and eventually entombed along with most of the passengers and crew.

Only the ten remained and they were an odd lot indeed. Young Cat, the cabin boy, wondered if and how they would be able to rise above their differences and pull together. Little did he realize what appalling physical and psychological conditions they would have to contend with as they struggled to keep alive on a bleak and forsaken island. Did they have the will and determination to survive?

Eth Clifford has created a compelling story of survival. Through young Cat Rider's eyes she explores with perception and sensitivity relationships within a group, when people suddenly thrust together in intimate interdependency have ... dividual courage, ingenuity, ... rely on.

The Curse of the Moonraker

∽

A Tale of Survival

Rosenberg, Ethel (Clifford)

ETH CLIFFORD, pseud.

Houghton Mifflin Company Boston 1977

Also by
ETH CLIFFORD

Burning Star
Search for the Crescent Moon
The Wild One
The Year of the Three-Legged Deer

Library of Congress Cataloging in Publication Data

Clifford, Eth, 1915–
The curse of the moonraker.

SUMMARY: The survivors of a strange shipwreck
in the Auckland Islands fight for survival under
seemingly hopeless conditions.
[1. Shipwrecks — Fiction. 2. Survival — Fiction]
I. Title.
PZ7.C62214Cu   [Fic]   77-24431
ISBN 0-395-25837-5

CONTENTS

This is for my dearest and best friend,
my husband, David Rosenberg,
who has been for me, through the years,
always
a man for all seasons

1

The Greenstone Jade

Gᴇᴛ ɪᴛ ʏᴏᴜʀsᴇʟꜰ!" Catlow Rider shouted. He could feel his rage spinning up from the tight knot in his stomach, spreading like a searing flame through his chest, burning up into his face, turning it red and hot.

Cat had done more than his share of tasks this day without complaint, had been doing them since the *Moonraker* had sailed from Melbourne, Australia, just nine days ago. As cabin boy on the square-rigger, his first duty, of course, was to serve the captain. But he'd been aloft in the rigging, dragging the royal and topgallant stunsails into the round tops and again to help shake the sails out, at least six times this day. Cat didn't mind that, though it was hard work. The small light stunsails, surging out in the freshening breezes, helped the *Moonraker* fairly fly across the water before the wind. Cat loved the feeling of speed; it was a heady sensation — this race with time. The *Moonraker* wasn't as fast as the clippers; still she was a good ship. But there was more to it than just serving the captain and going aloft. Between times he had been, as always, at the beck and call of the crew. In addition, he had brought food from the galley to the men on watch. And Slush, the cook, had found an endless and steady assortment of chores for Cat.

Slush was a thin, spare man, sun-wrinkled and sun-shriveled, with small, hard, raisin eyes, pinched lips, and a habit of twitching his head about like a dog sniffing a strange scent on the wind. Cat had helped Slush prepare the evening meal of lobscouse, peeling the potatoes and cutting up the salt meat while Slush, humming tunelessly, turned out a murky evil-smelling brown liquid called gravy. Then Cat had split open the hardtack with a knife and struck the biscuits sharply against the counter edge to dislodge the weevils before Slush threw the hardtack on top of the stew.

Now, after supper, having finished cleaning the plates and the pannikins, Cat had come up on deck, and there, sitting astride the water cask, was Rube Gullitt. Gullitt had called Cat and ordered him to get a drink of water. That was when the tired Cat rebelled.

"*What did you say?*" Rube Gullitt slid off the cask. He was a bold-looking man, with glittering black eyes and a thin nose that swooped down over his thin lips like a predatory bird.

"I said get it yourself," Cat repeated stubbornly, standing his ground. He didn't care what Rube Gullitt did now. The sight of Gullitt on the cask, too lazy or too mean to draw his own water, had been more than Cat could bear.

"Oh, now boy, you shouldn't have talked to me that

way," Gullitt said, angered. "No sirree, you shouldn't have talked to me that way at all." He covered the deck between Cat and himself in a few quick strides and knocked Cat down with a hard backsweep of his hand. Then he reached down and pulled Cat to his feet. "When I tell you something, Cat Rider, you hop! Understand?" He raised his hand, prepared to strike Cat again, and found his hand caught and held in midair in a tight grip.

"Let the boy go!" a voice said in Gullitt's ear.

"Stay out of this, Gray," Gullitt snapped, recognizing the voice of his fellow seaman.

"Not until you let the boy go," the other repeated, tightening his hold. Gullitt released his grip on Cat, who backed off, rubbing his face. It was only then that Spencer Gray, the seaman who had come to Cat's aid, dropped Gullitt's hand.

Cat thought Gray was the most handsome man he had ever seen. Gray had light amber eyes, outstanding in his honey-colored skin. He had the large straight nose, the high cheekbones, and the broad face typical of his mother's people, the Maoris of New Zealand. But his straight, sun-bleached fine fair hair, like his curiously light eyes and his name, Gray had once told Cat, was the gift of his English father.

"This is private, between me and the boy," Gullitt said. He was facing Gray now, in kind of a half crouch, swaying back and forth slightly, his fingers opening and closing.

Gullitt was going to force Gray into a fight, Cat thought. Quickly he said, "I'll get you the water, Mr. Gullitt."

I should have when he asked for it, Cat told himself, no matter how tired I was. After all, Cat knew very well that boys like himself and greenhorn sailors were fair game for the seasoned seamen. He'd known that from the first day he had set foot on the *Moonraker* in Boston, way back in November. The old year of 1865 had slipped by while the *Moonraker* was at sea, and now it was May, 1866. Cat had had time enough to learn a great deal about life aboard a square-rigger all those long months.

"Get out of the way, Cat," Gullitt said, keeping his eyes fixed on Gray. Cat noticed that Gray was running his hand back and forth across his chest. It was obvious that Gullitt had noticed the gesture, too. Spencer Gray must be nervous. That didn't surprise Cat. Gullitt had a quick mean temper and Gray was a peaceable man.

Suddenly, Rube Gullitt leaped forward and smashed his fist against the other man's mouth. Instantly, a thin red trickle of blood appeared in the corner of Gray's lips. Gullitt danced away, then came in close again. He lashed out at Gray's head in a feinting movement with his left hand and when Gray turned his head aside to avoid the blow, struck him hard in the stomach with his right fist.

Cat winced, as if the blow had been aimed at him.

Gray doubled over but came up from his crouch to land a sharp blow of his own, catching Gullitt just under the chin. Now it was Gray who moved closer. With a series of quick jabs, he drove Gullitt back against the rail. Gullitt leaned down as if he were falling. Gray stepped back.

"Watch out!" Cat cried. He had seen Gullitt reach for a knife, hidden in his boot. Now Gray saw it, too, as it glittered between them. Gullitt slashed out, missed, slashed again. This time it was Gray who retreated until he was stopped by the rail.

Cat was desperate. Usually, there were some crew members about. Now, strangely enough, the deck was deserted. He had to help Gray. But how? He looked about the deck frantically. If only he could find something, anything . . . his glance took in a belaying pin, moved on, came back. The belaying pin! Quietly, Cat moved away from the fighting men, seized the hard wooden piece and hefted it in his hand.

Gullitt's arm was high, the knife ready for the downward plunge. Timing his action carefully, Cat took aim and let the belaying pin fly. It caught Gullitt above the wrist, paralyzing his arm in midair. With a cry, Gullitt dropped the knife and began to rub his benumbed fingers.

"You're going to wish you'd never been born, Cat Rider," Gullitt swore, clutching his bruised wrist.

"You may yet have the same wish yourself," a deep voice said. In the gathering darkness, Gullitt had not seen the passenger approach. John Kell, the man who had spoken, was a long time away from Ireland, but the lilt of the brogue was still there. He was a tall, burly, black-bearded man with a keen look in his lively, intelligent dark eyes. His features were large but well formed. People warmed to him when he smiled, but when he was angry, as now, his face was forbidding. Although he had never served in an army, he had almost a military air, like a capable officer used to giving commands and expecting them to be obeyed. In any group, John Kell was a man who made his presence felt.

If Rube Gullitt was taken aback, he did not show it. "You're out of bounds here, mister," he rasped at Kell.

"I think not," Kell answered quietly. "With the gracious permission of Captain Laws, I have the run of the ship. Seeing that I was once by way of being a seaman myself, don't you know."

Sullenly, Gullitt stared at the two men and the boy. Then, without another word, he spun on his heel and left them.

"A word of advice, laddie," Kell told Cat seriously. "Be careful. You've made yourself a powerful enemy, and it's a long way between here and home. Boston, I think you mentioned, if I remember it right."

Cat sighed. "Boston. Yes, sir. In Massachusetts." And times like these, Cat thought, rubbing his face, he wished that he had never left that bustling seaport.

Standing beside Kell, Cat felt smaller than he actually was. Strong and wiry for his age, at thirteen he still had time to grow, but he knew that he would never achieve Kell's six-foot-four-inch well-muscled frame. Cat's fine opaline green eyes narrowed as he considered Kell's words about Gullitt. Yes. It would be a long, long time before the *Moonraker* touched American shores again. Now, nine days out of port, the *Moonraker* was running just south of the Snares Islands to catch the prevailing westerlies. Then the square-rigger would take the great circle route, sailing around the Cape, braving the big seas called the Cape Horn greybeards, and then head for London. From London, the *Moonraker* would set sail for America. And in London,

Cat's two good defenders, Kell and Gray, would debark, Kell to return to Ireland, and Gray to sign on to another ship. Then who would protect Cat from Gullitt?

"You've got to stay out of Gullitt's way," Gray said.

"There's nothing I'd like better," Cat replied fervently, "but he seeks me out."

From the time Cat had first come aboard in Boston, Gullitt had played cat-and-mouse with him. He had grabbed Cat's seabag, pretending to be helpful, and had dropped it into a tub of bilge water on the lower deck while the other seamen had looked on grinning. Anger stained Cat's face red, but he knew better than to complain, for Gullitt was laughing, and the other seamen, laughing too, were watching Cat carefully. Without a word, Cat had rolled up his sleeve and plunged his arm into the slimy water, turning his head away and trying to keep from gagging at the stench that rose from the tub. When he pulled his seabag to the surface finally, everything in it was soaked through.

Captain Laws had been passing by. Luxurious sideburns, mustache and beard blended together on the captain's face, so that all one could see were his eyes and nose. He appeared to have no lips at all. When he spoke, the words seemed to spill forth from a small dark opening hidden in the thick hair.

"Welcome aboard, son," the captain said drily. He did not censure the men. If the boy was to survive the life at sea, he'd have to toughen up, and he might as well start toughening up at once. The captain walked on, then turned. "There's clean water in that other tub," he pointed. "Get your things washed."

"Aye, aye, sir," Cat answered.

And that had been his introduction to Rube Gullitt.

Kell and Gray listened gravely to Cat's story.

"Sure, and it seems to be the way of things," Kell sighed. "Especially aboard a ship. There are some that play these cat-and-mouse games. I've seen it time and again . . . the mean-spirited and their cruel little ways. If you can't stand the gaff, laddie, you'd best be seeking another way of life."

Cat set his lips obstinately. "No, sir. I'm a seaman. I'm only a cabin boy now, but someday I'll be a captain, with my own ship."

Kell clapped his hand on Cat's shoulder. "Stout lad." He turned to Gray. "It would not be amiss for you yourself to be on the lookout for our friend Gullitt, I'm thinking."

"I've met a few Gullitts in my time." Gray smiled faintly. "I've learned to be careful." Without thinking, Gray stroked his chest again.

"Why do you do that, Mr. Gray?" Cat asked impulsively. "You rubbed your chest before the fight, too."

Kell had seen the gesture, too. "I think, Cat, that our friend Mr. Gray has a charm against evil round his neck. Am I right? A Maori charm? I've heard some talk of it whilst I've lived in New Zealand. A beautiful stone, they say, shaped like a tear drop."

Gray pulled the amulet from around his neck to show it to Kell and Cat. "Feel it," he urged. As first Cat and then Kell stroked the stone, Gray smiled. "Now you will have good fortune for what is left of this day. If you touch the stone in the morning, you will have good fortune all that day."

"I've heard that the stone is so hard it can't be crushed or even scratched." Kell examined the stone intently. "It's a beautiful stone, right enough." The base of the stone was dark; its green color lightened toward the center and seemed almost white at the tip.

Cat ran his fingers along the cord from which the stone was suspended. It seemed to give off a faint and delicately sweet scent.

"These braids have a nice smell." Cat sniffed in the fragrance.

"They are made from spear grass. As you can see, there are seven braids," Gray explained.

"Seven being a lucky number," Kell remembered.

"You seem to know much about the Maoris. Do you know the story of our greenstone jade?" Gray asked.

"I don't," Cat interrupted eagerly. "I'd like to hear it. Please, Mr. Gray. I'd like very much to hear it."

The two men and Cat had moved to stand beside the rail. A light mist, just beginning to form, drifted slowly toward the ship, touching their faces, settling quietly around them.

"Once," Gray began, staring dreamily across the rail, "even before my grandfather's grandfather's time, longer ago than that, a strange affliction came upon my people. Some evil ones among my people had enraged Kai-Alua, the god of vengeance. In a blaze of temper, he spread among my people a disease that wasted them away. Soon the dead outnumbered the living. Those who lived were so weak they could not bury the dead, and so their bodies lay on the ground to be picked clean by birds of prey. It was a time of great, of overwhelming sorrow.

"The goddess of mercy pleaded with Kai-Alua, and she wept for us. Seeing our distress, she wept without ceasing. Her tears fell to earth like droplets of warm rain, soaking the ground, sinking deeper and deeper until the tears washed through the greenstone lying far below. The tears of the goddess of mercy held all the sorrow of my people, and this sorrow penetrated the greenstone jade. The weight of the tears fell to the bottom of the jade. For that reason the base of the greenstone is darker than the top."

Gray paused. "I do not know if either of you has ever dived deep into the ocean. The deeper one goes, the darker the water is. In the depth of the ocean there is *po*, which is blackness. But as one turns and swims upward, the blackness is left behind; the water becomes greener and ever greener. Then at last one reaches *Ao*, the light that shines on the surface of the water." He looked at Cat earnestly. "My people say that if there was no night, one could not glory in the coming of dawn. If one did not shed tears, how could one know the delight of laughter? To know joy, one must first know sorrow.

"This stone," Gray said, his fingers caressing the amulet, "which we call the water of tears, was given to me by my mother as she lay dying. She took it from around her neck and placed it around mine. 'Rub the stone each day,' she told me, 'and no harm will come to you that day. You will suffer,' she said, 'and your heart will have its grief, but this you must accept, for you can never know what true happiness is until you have lived with sorrow first.' And she was right. I have known sorrow and I have known joy."

10

"And you wear the stone always, day and night?" Cat asked.

Gray nodded. "Day and night. I am never without it."

"And no harm can come to the wearer of the greenstone jade?" Cat said, stroking the amulet and then returning it to Gray, who immediately slipped his head through the braided grass necklet.

"No harm," Gray replied firmly. "The greenstone jade is a symbol of life. That is why it is sacred to our people."

"I wish I had a stone like yours," Cat said wistfully. "Slush keeps saying this is an ill-omened ship."

"Ill-omened, is it?" Kell was amused. "Now why would that be, laddie? Though sailors find omens in all manner of things," he added. "I can testify to that."

"Well," Cat began, "our second day out of Boston we were hit by a gale, and the third mate was washed overboard while the crew was shortening sail. And then in Melbourne, we took on the cargo meant for the clipper *London*."

"The *London* sank in the Bay of Biscay," Gray told Kell.

"And Slush said when we did that, we signed our own doom," Cat continued. "Good as dead, all of us, Slush said. And then there's the gold."

Kell's interest quickened. "What about the gold?"

"Everyone on board knows the *Moonraker* carries more than four thousand ounces of gold. I've seen the boxes," Cat said. "There are four of them, square wooden boxes bound in iron. Slush says those four boxes alone are worth more than a quarter of a million dollars, and he says that doesn't even take in the parcels of gold the miners have hidden in their cabins. Slush says that much gold is cursed."

"I've just come from the goldfields, as have most of the passengers aboard. There's no curse on the gold, lad. Gold is no more nor no less than what use people make of it, don't you see. He's an evil-croaking bird, that one," Kell said with strong distaste, "filling your head with his warnings and portents. You're a sensible lad. You'll not tell me you take the man's blathering seriously."

"I guess not," Cat said, but he seemed doubtful.

Gray touched the amulet. The boy had saved his life. Gullitt would surely have killed him, and now Cat would pay for his brave action one way or another, for Rube Gullitt was not a man to forget a grudge. On impulse, Gray took the amulet from his neck and thrust it into Cat's hand.

"Oh, no sir!" Cat was shocked. "I can't take this."

"I can get another."

"But what will you do meanwhile?" Cat asked anxiously.

"Why I will come to you every morning," Gray answered lightly, "and I will rub my fingers across the jade, and then I, too, will be safe."

Still Cat worried. "Are you sure?"

"I am sure."

Kell looked at Gray, started to speak, and fell silent. He knew that Gray truly believed in the power of the greenstone jade.

Cat sighed. It was a beautiful story, the legend of the greenstone. He wondered if one had to be a Maori to be protected. But even if he had no Maori blood, he nonetheless felt curiously comforted by the amulet, slipping it on so that it could rest smooth and warm against his chest.

"No harm can come to me now," Cat repeated slowly.

"You must remember that always," Gray said seriously. "No harm can ever come to the wearer of the greenstone jade."

2

Graveyard of the Sea

Cat woke from a restless sleep, his mind struggling loose from a chain of oppressive dreams. He could hear his heart beating, a quick thrumming bursting noise in his ears. He opened his eyes wide but he made no attempt to get up. Instead, he turned his head to one side and listened intently. He thought he had heard a shout. There! It came again!

"Land on the port bow!" That was Reid Willis, the lookout Captain Laws had posted forward after the fog had closed in on the *Moonraker*. For two days and two nights now fog had wrapped itself about the square-rigger, a heavy gray mist so thick, Slush had muttered, that you could walk on it. Even Kell had been uneasy.

"We're like a phantom ship sailing a ghostly sea," he

had said, and then, seeing Cat's expression, had laughed and added, "Pay me no mind, lad. It was standing on deck and barely making out the end of the jib boom that put the fanciful notion in my head."

Land on the port bow? Cat puzzled. There must be some mistake. There had been no sightings during the past two days and nights of fog. Had the weather cleared while Cat had been below? Cat rubbed his eyes hard, trying to come completely awake. The captain would be wanting his coffee; Captain Laws was almost never without a cup of that bitter brew in his hands. Cat made his way to the galley, then searched out the captain, who had posted himself on the weatherside of the ship, peering intently into the darkness.

"I've brought your coffee," Cat began, but the captain waved him aside brusquely.

"What do you see, Mr. Chance?" the captain called. The first mate, who had scaled the lower mizzen rigging, shook his head. Then, realizing that the captain could barely see him, called, "All I can make out is a dark shape, sir. It could be land. But more likely it's a fog bank."

"Whatever it is, I want no part of it. I want all hands to their stations!"

Omar Chance dropped down from the rigging. "What's your reckoning, sir?"

Captain Laws stroked his beard thoughtfully.

"If it's land, we're probably sighting the northern-most island of the Aucklands. Square away the yards," he commanded as the crew scrambled to their stations.

The seamen fell to their tasks briskly and soon the square-rigger was running well before the wind, her sails billowing. She bore away northward for a time and then hauled up again to the east.

"She's cleared the land," Chance reported with relief. Chance was a slender, silent man with a grave-looking face and unsmiling eyes, a quiet man who listened more than he spoke.

The captain grunted. "My coffee," he said with sudden irritation. "Where did that blasted boy go with my coffee?"

Cat had disappeared. He was on his way to the galley with the cold coffee, knowing the captain would be demanding a hot drink, the hotter the better, once the crisis was past. He kept turning and glancing about as he ran his errand, hoping he might spot John Kell. Maybe Kell could explain to Cat why the captain believed they were running so close to the Auckland Islands. How could the square-rigger be so far off course? The Auckland Islands were almost three hundred miles south of New Zealand!

Cat thought about John Kell as he reached the galley, filled the captain's cup, and then carried the coffee to the bridge. It was more than size that made John Kell so confident. There were many men on board who were easily as tall as Kell. Maybe it was the life Kell had led since he had left Ireland when he was eighteen years old. That was more than twenty years ago, Kell had told Cat. His wanderings had taken him far from home to some wild and rough places, to the wilderness of New Zealand on its west coast, to the goldfields in Australia. John Kell had been many things — adventurer, seaman, river pilot, gold prospector. He was strong. The strength was in his height; it was in the broad shoulders and the powerful body. But it was more than that. It was also in his eyes.

Cat arrived on the bridge in time to hear Reid Willis cry, *"Land on our starboard bow!"* These words chased every other thought from Cat's mind. The captain, reaching for the cup, drained it without noticing or caring what it contained. His mind, too, was occupied with uneasy thoughts.

"What do you spy through the glass, Mr. Chance?" he asked abruptly.

"It has the appearance of another fog bank, about three or four miles distant on our lee beam."

The captain thrust the empty cup back into Cat's hands. "Filthy stuff," he complained absently. "Let me have that glass, Mr. Chance."

Cat waited, not wanting to leave, anxious to learn what the captain might see through the glass, but the captain dismissed him irritably. "Go below, boy."

Suddenly a sense of weariness swept over Cat. Seven bells had sounded. It was now 11:30 P.M., time enough for him to be in bed. He headed below gratefully, stretched out on his bunk, and closed his eyes. But sleep would not come. He tossed and turned, from one side to another, onto his back, and then face down. But when the restlessness became overwhelming, he rose and went back up on deck, where he hung over the rail, squinting his eyes into narrow slits, trying to see what lay ahead on the lee beam.

"I expect that was Disappointment Island," John Kell said from out of the darkness. When Cat jumped, Kell patted his arm reassuringly. "It's only Kell here. And MacCool O'Shea as well," he added, as another shape formed beside them in the fog. The second man was not so tall as John Kell nor as lean. He was square-built, with short powerful arms and rough strong hands. "We couldn't sleep. I met young Billy Smithy just coming off watch. I asked him what the captain thought our bearing was, and it seems the captain thinks we're just off Disappointment Island."

"Disappointment Island?" O'Shea echoed. "Are you saying . . ." He broke off to stare at Kell with growing apprehension in his eyes. "Why man dear, that's one of the Auckland group. It's treacherous waters we're in, to be sure, if the captain is right."

O'Shea had heard many tales . . . what had one seaman called this area? He had it now. A graveyard, the man had said straight out, a graveyard for ships. O'Shea shuddered.

"Curse this place," he cried, "and curse the sea." He turned to Cat. "Some men love the sea, but MacCool O'Shea isn't one of them, you've my word on that! Do you think I'd have set foot on board a ship at all if I could have reached Australia and the goldfields any other way? Not MacCool O'Shea, I promise you. I jumped ship in Australia," he added, reminiscently. "Swam half a mile to shore I did, with every stitch I owned in the world in a pack on my head and my only pair of boots hanging round my neck."

For a moment Cat forgot about the fog and the threat of danger ahead.

"How were you able to jump ship, Mr. O'Shea?" he asked with interest. "Wasn't a watch posted?"

"Bless the lad! Was a watch posted, he asks." O'Shea grinned. "To be sure, there was a watch indeed. But I waited until the wee small hours, don't you see, and then, when they were weary and the way was clear, I slid down the anchor chain. Not the easiest way to leave a ship, mind. And then of course once I was on land, it was touch and go for almost a week, with me hiding out from troopers searching for deserters. There was many a one like me with the fever in him for the gold. And plenty of gold is stored aboard this very ship, as well you know."

Cat nodded. "Slush says there are fine jewels somewhere aboard as well."

"Jewels, is it?" O'Shea jeered. "Worth a king's ransom no doubt he's been telling you. Well then, it's a true treasure ship we're sailing, right enough."

Kell asked them, sharply, to be quiet. He had turned his head and was listening intently. Then Cat and O'Shea heard the cry from the lookout.

"Land! Dead ahead!"

"Land!" O'Shea's voice shook. "Dead ahead, the man says." He put his hand on Kell's arm. "Aye, that's the proper word for it. For we're good as dead if we run into it."

"The captain's as able a man as any who ever commanded a ship," Kell said soothingly. "Now even if it is land ahead, and not a fog bank, the captain is probably aiming to sail between Disappointment Island and Desolation Island. The captain's already hauled the ship on port tack." O'Shea groaned. "Never mind, MacCool." Kell laughed. O'Shea was not a man for nautical language.

"Disappointment Island. Desolation Island," O'Shea

repeated dolefully. "You'd not call those names to lift a man's spirit."

Cat had not been following the exchange between the two men for he had become aware of something that neither Kell nor O'Shea had as yet noticed.

"Mr. Kell, sir," Cat broke in urgently. "Listen!" His strong feeling of unease communicated itself to the men; it made the other two fall silent.

"Devil take it," O'Shea cried out at last. "What am I listening for?"

What did Cat hear? He himself could hear only the seas crashing against rocks. Rocks! Was that it, then? Rocks meant a shore. What waited for them was land and not a fog bank. O'Shea shuddered.

"I can't hear the wind," Cat whispered, apprehensively. "The wind is dying down."

"What of that?" O'Shea replied impatiently. "We're moving well enough."

It was true. The *Moonraker* was gathering way but it was the heavy swells beneath her that were pushing her steadily onward. Now, even as Cat spoke, the sails were beginning to slacken and go limp.

"Look to the sails," Cat bid them. "There's no wind."

"But I felt a puff of air just then. Did you feel it, Johnnie? There it goes again! Lift your head, man. Do you not feel it?" O'Shea appealed to Kell.

Captain Laws had long since ordered every sail to be set and every yard braced to catch any errant capful of wind. A sail lifted briefly and then sagged. Not the faintest quiver of air stirred. The square-rigger was setting bodily toward a towering cliff, where the hostile rocks waited.

"So the seaman was right," O'Shea muttered, speaking his thoughts aloud, "this *is* the graveyard of the sea."

"Be quiet, MacCool," Kell said sharply, looking at Cat.

But the damage was done. Cat was staring at O'Shea, his eyes wide with shock. O'Shea's words ran round and round in Cat's head. Graveyard, Cat's mind whispered. This is the graveyard of the sea.

3

Devil Astride the Ship

THERE WAS SILENCE, and there was sound. The louder the sound of the sea, the thicker the silence on board the *Moonraker*. At first there had been a flurry of activity for the captain had issued clear orders: All passengers were to be summoned aft; the passengers were not to stop for anything, the captain emphasized to the crew; the captain wanted everyone on deck, now, at once.

Cat, running past Kell and O'Shea, on his way below deck, turned and called back the captain's instructions as he hurried on his errand.

O'Shea stared after Cat, then cried out hoarsely,

"The gold! Our gold!" He left Kell hastily, running, ignoring Kell's shout, "Let it go, man! It's no use to us now."

Cat could not believe what he saw below. In cabin after cabin, miners were yanking blankets from their bunks, filling them with their hidden gold, and tying the blankets with anxious, trembling hands.

"Please, sir," Cat said, time after time, "the captain wants everyone on deck at the rear of the ship." For what did *aft* mean, after all, to dazed and hysterical landlubbers?

Some of the miners stared at him without understanding. Others pushed him aside roughly, intent on saving their gold. The few women passengers clutched their children, or made feeble attempts to pack some of their clothing. But with the help of other crew members, Cat finally managed to herd the passengers on deck. They huddled in groups, the women keeping tight rein on their children, the miners clenching their blankets so hard the veins stood out on their hands. But all were silent. An uncanny hush, a tomblike quiet, embraced the ship.

And all the while, ceaselessly, the choppy waters continued to nudge the *Moonraker* forward, aiming her toward the waiting cliff that rose a sharp four hundred feet into the air.

Strangely, though the sea was swift, the square-rigger moved slowly, reluctantly, an unwilling partner in this dance of death. Once a fast-moving tide caught her up and swung her south away from the cliff. But the sea was wayward and savage. Another eddy snatched the ship and hurried her north again. To the crew, time seemed to move in agonizing droplets of seconds. To the passengers, time went by swift as water through open hands, rushing them too soon to the waiting silent mountain in the sea.

"Mother of God!" a voice said behind Cat. It was Slush, his eyes wild with fear. "Why can't it be done and over with?"

Cat's hand flew to his amulet.

"You and that precious stone," Slush growled. "It won't save you now."

Hard on his words, the jib boom slammed against rocks jutting out from the base of the cliff. A violent shudder ran through the frame of the square-rigger. There was a sharp snapping sound as the jib boom and bowsprit were torn from the ship and whipped away in the roiling waters.

The angry sea was not done. Now it took the *Moonraker* and spun her around, driving her back until her stern smashed against still another projection of rocks. The rudder flew apart. The spanker boom cracked and fell, killing several miners and pinning the helmsman to the wheel. His retching cry of pain as his ribs broke was lost in the screams of the terrified passengers.

Cat was thrown to the deck; his head struck the hard wood. For a moment, he slipped into a rushing tunnel of darkness. He felt hands at his throat, a quick brushing motion, and then someone calling his name.

"Cat! Cat! That's it! Sit up, boy. You'll be all right in a minute."

Cat sat up and felt the back of his head gingerly. It felt sore to the touch, but the dizziness that had made his head spin and turned his stomach queazy was beginning to pass.

"Mr. Gray." Cat struggled to his feet. "Thank you. I'm all right now." He looked around. "Slush was here a second ago," he said, puzzled. "He was talking to me . . ." Cat broke off in mid-sentence. "The greenstone jade," he stammered. "It's gone."

For a long moment, he stared at Spencer Gray. He's taken it back, Cat thought. He's taken back the greenstone jade. Spencer Gray returned Cat's look steadily, as if he knew what Cat was thinking. Ashamed, Cat dropped his glance.

"I'm sorry," he said lamely, without mentioning why he was apologizing.

"I would not take the amulet away, once I had given it," Gray said gravely.

"I know. I'm sorry," Cat said again. "It must have been Slush . . ." His voice trailed off.

"We will get it back for you," Gray promised.

They stood together, and, like the others on the ship, stared numbly at the cliff that now towered over them.

"We're going to die, aren't we, Mr. Gray?" Cat said. The ship would bear down hard upon the rocks and would split apart. All that would mark her passing would be bits and pieces of floating wreckage. He realized suddenly that he was trembling. It was fear, but it was also anger. He'd never be captain of his own ship now. Never. It's not fair, his mind cried. It's not fair.

Busy with his own thoughts, it was a moment before

he understood that something was happening. He turned his head and stared up at Gray who was staring ahead with widened eyes. Gray gasped, a sharp intake of breath, and caught Cat by the shoulder.

"Look there!" He pointed with outstretched arm, a smile beginning to touch his lips. "Look hard!"

At first Cat was speechless. Then he grabbed Gray's hand, pumping it up and down, wild with excitement.

"It's a cove, Mr. Gray," he shouted. "It's a cove! It's not one cliff, but two. And we're drifting right between them!"

The ship moved between the cliffs as if following a charted course. Cat stared up in awe at the precipices that hemmed in the ship as she was borne deeper into the inlet by the fast-moving current. Hard as he looked, he could not see where the somber towering cliffs peaked.

The heavy swells were urging the square-rigger farther and farther forward into the inlet. Suddenly, without warning, the ship was plunged into total darkness. In the abruptness of the raven-black eclipse, the violent grinding of the sides of the ship against the rigid walls became magnified.

Taken by surprise, passengers and crew alike fell momentarily silent. Then, in that uneasy ebony stillness, Cat recognized Billy Smithy's voice. Billy was a few years older than Cat, just nineteen, but already an able-bodied seaman. Billy was droning, "I don't want to die in the dark! I don't want to die in the dark! Please, God! Don't let me die in the dark!"

Prickles of icy dread ran up and down Cat's spine.

Billy's lament seemed to sweep through the ship. Now others cried out.

"For God's sake! Where are we? What's happening? Give us some light! Why can't we have light?"

Above the terrified calls, Captain Laws could be heard shouting for lanterns to be hung over the sides of the ship. Lamps were lit hastily and strung like shining beads over the rails. At first Cat was only aware of the dark mass of rock looming over them. He sent his glance searching up and down the smooth volcanic walls. Why not even a bird could find a resting place anywhere on these sleek flat surfaces, Cat thought despondently.

A deep longing for home so overwhelmed him that he could feel the tears ready to well up in his eyes. He remembered with fierce nostalgia the tiny black-capped chickadee that had nested in the hollow tree near his window back home in Boston. He could almost see the small active bird with its round chubby body and hear its lively chirping — *chickadee, dee dee dee.* He used to imitate the call, hanging out the window, trying to pinpoint the bird hiding in the foliage. Sometimes the bird trilled a quick bright reply — *chickadee, dee dee dee.*

Cat didn't realize that he had pursed his lips and was calling until MacCool O'Shea said in amazement, "We're minutes away from the briny and you're *whistling?*"

"Look up, MacCool," said John Kell quietly, "and you may well whistle too."

Cat tilted his head, as did O'Shea, and studied the cliffs again. Instantly, the bird vanished from his mind. In the dim light thrown off by the lanterns, Cat now saw what John Kell had discovered just minutes ago. O'Shea pursed his lips, letting a small hissing sound escape.

"The cliffs have closed over our heads!"

4

The Mortal Blow

Iᴛ's ᴀ ᴄᴀᴠᴇ! We're in a cave!" Cat's voice was shrill with shock. He had never heard of a cave in the sea. Caves were holes in the earth; they had long dank twisting tunnels and were filled with strange rock formations. As if in answer to the half-formed thoughts running through Cat's mind, Kell said, "It's a monster of a cave for sure that can take in an entire ship from the height of her mainmast and the breadth of her main yard."

"A sea cavern," O'Shea repeated. "A monstrous sea cavern."

"The captain will launch the boats," Cat said positively.

John Kell shook his head. "It would be mad to launch boats in the dark in this heavy swell," he said gently.

Though Kell did not know it, Captain Laws had already come to the same conclusion. A sounding had been taken. There were several fathoms under the stern, more than enough water to cover the *Moonraker.* Sick at heart, the ship out of his control, Captain Laws had to stand by helplessly as the *Moonraker* continued to push on further into the cave.

The nightmare went on. The fore royalmast ground into the overhanging rock and came crashing down, the sound of its fall echoing in the cave. Soon other spars followed. The topmast and lower mast were torn and splintered. The force of their fall drove the stump of one mast clear through the fo'c's'le deck. Another pierced the starboard deckhouse. And now huge masses of stone broke loose from the cliffs and came down in a deadly rain, broken spars mixed with the hurtling rocks.

"The devil himself is astride the ship," O'Shea lamented.

He and Kell and Cat had fled to join the other passengers and crew huddled together aft, trying to escape the crashing masts. Now there was another grinding noise that vibrated in their ears. It was the stump of the mainmast, catching against the solid rock roof.

"We're not moving, Mr. Kell," Cat whispered. "Is that good or bad?" he asked anxiously.

Kell shrugged. "Who's to know, lad?"

"Will he be launching the boats now do you think, Johnnie?"

"Now how can I speak for the captain, MacCool? My guess, for what it's worth, is that the captain will wait until daylight before ever he makes up his mind what to do next." Kell struck a match and lit his pipe.

"The wind is rising," O'Shea said. "Is that good or

bad?" he asked, unconsciously echoing the words Cat had used moments before.

"Bad, MacCool. Very bad." Kell bit on the stem of his pipe. The wind, now when the *Moonraker* needed it least, was bringing with it heavy rolls of sea. With every billow, the seams below the ship opened a little wider, the hull settled deeper and deeper into the water. The masts began to grate fretfully against the unyielding rock roof above.

"It's the darkness," O'Shea said, as much to comfort himself as the others. "You'll see. Things will look different in the morning."

Cat seized upon this, agreeing, "Everything's always so much worse at night. The captain will take action as soon as there's light."

"Yes," Kell said. "We'll be abandoning ship at dawn."

Abandoning ship? Abandon this beautiful proud ship? Cat mourned deep within himself. Why even the Melbourne newspapers had written about her. He'd seen an account in the *Argus*. Magnificent, the paper had said. A new ship of high class order, well-built of oak, copper and iron fastened, classed A-1 at Lloyd's of London.

"Aye," O'Shea agreed. "We'll be leaving her. She's about beaten her life out in this cave."

The *Moonraker* was dying, Cat thought. For a moment, he forgot about the eighty-three people aboard and the danger they were in, of the peril he was in. The beautiful ship was dying. Putting his arms across his knees, hugging them to his body, Cat stared bleakly into space. His obvious misery touched Kell, who reached out and pulled Cat close. "You've a right to grieve, Cat. There's much to grieve for."

The sober bone-blackness of the cavern began to yield slowly to tentative streaks of gray. Slowly the first hint of dawn appeared.

"It's getting on to daylight," O'Shea muttered. "We'll be taking to the boats soon."

"He can't wait much longer," Kell agreed. As if Kell's words were a signal, the mizzen topgallant mast toppled. While the roar of its crash still echoed, Captain Laws shouted for a spar and tackle to be rigged over the stern. Some lines and an iron kedge to be used as an anchor were placed in one of the quarterboats. Then carefully, very carefully, the quarterboat was launched.

"You, Gullitt. Willis. Smithy." Captain Laws ordered. "Into the first quarterboat. Pull her outside and see if a landing can be made outside the cave."

The three able-bodied seamen slid gingerly down into the quarterboat. The craft bobbed dangerously in the rough water, and it took all the skill of the three men to keep the boat from smashing into the square-rigger.

The captain shouted after them that the lines would be needed to haul out the other boats, and that he wanted the men to come back for the passengers after they had searched out a landing place. But the captain's words were lost in the howl of the wind.

Aboard the *Moonraker*, passengers and crew stared longingly after the quarterboat as the three men rowed hard toward the gaping jagged opening of the cave.

"I hope they find a landing place," O'Shea said prayerfully.

"It's not likely in this nasty sea," Kell replied.

"Then they'll be back to pick up passengers," O'Shea went on.

Cat was swept with a feeling of despair.

"No, sir," he said in a low voice. "They won't come back."

"Whisht, now!" O'Shea stared down at Cat with stern disapproval. "Are you saying they'd abandon us? Or abandon the women and children aboard?" He grew angrier as he spoke. "The captain told them plain as day . . ." He broke off. "Are you telling me seamen would disobey their captain's orders?"

"No, sir. They won't. That's why they won't come back." Cat was insistent. "They were ordered to pull outside and that's where they'll stay, because they didn't hear the rest of the captain's command."

O'Shea turned and appealed to Kell. "The boy's gone daft. Why would three able-bodied men sit out there, alone in a boat that could hold ten or more people, when there are passengers to be rescued?"

"No matter, MacCool," Kell replied quietly. "The captain realizes what has happened. He's just ordered the second quarterboat made ready. Look there. See? Provisions are being put on her now."

Already a quantity of salt pork and about fifty cans of preserved meat had been placed in the second quarterboat. Now the captain looked about, making his decision as to who would man the boat.

"Mr. Chance," the captain called.

The first mate stepped to his side. "Aye, aye, captain."

"You and Gray and John Kell — he's a strong man.

Into the quarterboat and hold her steady to take on passengers."

"Aye, aye, sir," Chance repeated.

Kell, moving away from O'Shea and Cat, hesitated briefly.

"It will be women and children first," he said, looking at Cat soberly. "You may be able to get onto the longboat when the captain gets ready to launch her."

Cat was afraid. He could not remember ever having been this afraid before — a fear that swept over him in steady chilling waves and at the same time made the palms of his hands sweat and beads of perspiration rim his upper lip. His face was pale, seeming whiter than usual in contrast to his black hair. His almost vertical black pupils seemed just slits of darkness, lost in the green iris of his eyes. He had to fight down a feeling of nausea. But his voice was steady when he replied.

"I'm a seaman, Mr. Kell. I know women and children come first."

The second quarterboat was launched carefully. Chance, Gray, and Kell held it as steady as they could in the turbulent water. This time Captain Laws made certain he was heard.

"Mr. Chance," he called. "The women and children are to be rowed out to the other quarterboat and transferred. You will then come back for additional passengers."

"Aye, aye, sir," Chance shouted back.

Captain Laws turned to face the people on board the ship. "I want the women and children to step forward. Quickly, please, ladies." He listened to the shuddering of the hull, the screaming protest of the ship's timbers.

The cavern was a giant echo chamber, and every sound bounced off the walls and howled its way back to the ship. "Ladies," he said impatiently. "Step forward."

Cat watched with disbelief as he saw that the women remained frozen where they were, refusing to leave the *Moonraker*. They had looked down at the water below, at the quarterboat tossing and turning, and at the men working to keep her fairly close to the square-rigger, and were terrified. They clung to the crippled ship.

"It's suicide to leave the ship," one woman cried out at last.

"Madam," Captain Laws said, trying to remain calm, "it is most certain death to remain."

Cat's eyes moved from one woman's face to another, searching. He was looking for Mrs. Taylor, a widow who was going home to Ireland. Cat had found her interesting with her stories about the goldminers who had stayed at her boarding house in Melbourne on the way back from the goldfields. She had a good sense of humor and laughed easily. Cat liked her, liked her plain appealing face, her smoke-gray eyes, her broad smile, her whispery voice.

Spotting her in the crowd, Cat moved quickly to her side.

"Mrs. Taylor," he called urgently.

She turned and waited for him to speak.

"Please, Mrs. Taylor," Cat begged. "You go first. The other women will follow."

"I'm to be the leader of the flock then?" she asked. She shook her head. "I think not." Seeing his eyes cloud with disappointment, she added gently, "I can't swim, Cat. I'd not be much of an example, drowning in front of their eyes."

"They won't let you drown. Please, Mrs. Taylor." He caught her hand. "Somebody has to show the others it's all right to leave the ship."

Mrs. Taylor studied Cat for a moment, then the women clutching their children, and Captain Laws, impatient, concerned, and helpless before the women's determination not to be saved.

She shrugged.

"I might as well drown now as later," she told Cat, moving briskly from his side to step directly before the captain. His eyes lit when she came forward.

"I can't swim," she told him guardedly, in a low voice, so the others could not overhear. "But if you think it will help, captain, I'll go over the side."

"Here's a splendid beginning!" the captain called, in a ringing voice. He whispered, "Don't be frightened when you hit the water. You'll be safe, I promise." Fearful that she might change her mind, the captain summoned a sailor and ordered brusquely, "Secure a rope around the lady's waist, seaman."

"Aye, aye, sir." He tied the rope around her, speaking soothingly as he did so. "You'll be fine, ma'am. You'll be fine."

When he stepped back after tying the rope, two crewmen lifted her easily and dropped her carefully into the frothing sea. As the women on board watched with horrified eyes, she disappeared beneath the water. But the sailors, playing the rope, brought her sputtering up to the surface quickly.

Kell called to her, encouraging her to swim toward the quarterboat.

"I can't swim," she called back faintly. At once, Kell dove into the water; swimming toward her with long powerful strokes, he seized her and pulled her toward the quarterboat, where willing hands lifted her aboard. Feeling calmer now that her initial panic in the water had subsided, she called to the women to follow her, waving her hand and smiling, but still they clung to their children and shook their heads wordlessly.

Up to this moment, things had moved in an orderly fashion. Suddenly, a wave of panic seemed to seize everyone on board. The passengers fought one another for a place in the longboat, which had not yet been launched. Men hurled themselves overboard, aiming for the boat waiting below in the water, and vanished. Miners looked on with dazed expressions and clutched their gold in rigid hands. Others climbed the rigging of the broken mizzenmast.

MacCool O'Shea slid down a line, and was swallowed by the water. He struggled upward and swam steadily until Kell was able to pull him, gasping for breath, into the boat.

Cat, stunned by the pandemonium that surrounded him, stood in an almost dreamlike state, wondering what to do. Slush raced by and leaped over the rail. Cat, realizing at last that it was now everyone for himself, followed Slush. Cat disappeared in the water, rose again, and glanced about anxiously, not sure at first where he was. Then he saw the quarterboat; he struck out resolutely for it, but the heavy swells fought him. Each time he advanced, another roller pushed him back.

I can't reach it, he thought. I can't. I'm going to die here, in this terrible place. This wouldn't be happening if I still had the greenstone jade, he mourned. He felt himself drifting. He forced himself to keep his attention on the boat. I won't give up, he said fiercely. I won't. Then he felt himself being lifted and a voice spoke words of encouragement in his ear.

"Swim, laddie, swim for all you're worth!" John Kell was at his side, steadying him and propelling him toward the quarterboat, where Spencer Gray reached down and pulled him to safety. Gray leaned over the side again, meaning to help Kell climb aboard, but his hands were seized instead by Slush, so exhausted by the battle with the billows that he now hung limply from Gray's hands. Kell pushed him from beneath; Slush fell into the boat like a hooked fish, body quivering and mouth gaping. Kell then swung himself aboard.

Cat looked back at the *Moonraker*. At that moment a huge wave, larger than any that had yet swept into the cavern, caught the ship and hurled her upward. The impact of the stump of the mainmast against the roof drove the lower end of the stump clear through the bottom of the ship. This was the final, the mortal blow. The *Moonraker* began to sink rapidly. Now the waves washed freely across her deck. One enormous swell caught the longboat and floated her free of the dying ship.

"Mr. Chance," Kell urged. "We'd best row clear of the ship or she'll pull us down with her."

Chance agreed. "We'll pull off a way and wait. We may be able to pick up quite a few of the passengers."

"I don't see the captain on the longboat," Cat said anxiously.

"There are so many on the boat it's hard to see who's on it," O'Shea replied.

As if she had waited to see the boats clear, the *Moonraker* was now suddenly submerged. For a few moments, only her mizzen-topmast crosstrees still remained visible. There, two figures could be seen. One was a miner gone quite mad, a package under one arm, shouting, "Save the gold I say! Save the gold!"

The other was Captain Laws.

"Stop!" Chance ordered. "We've got to go back for the captain. I will not abandon the captain!"

Kell said gently, "It's too late, Mr. Chance. Don't you see, man? It's too late."

"Aye," O'Shea said huskily, "the brave man has chosen to go down with his ship."

Cat turned away, and now he wept, openly and unashamedly.

5

The Desperate Search

The *Moonraker* was gone. All that remained now were the three boats — the first quarterboat just outside the cave; the second holding Cat and the others, which had removed itself far enough from the *Moonraker* to get free

of her downward tug; and the longboat, overcowded
with passengers and crew, far more than it could
reasonably hold. And yet the longboat began to make
progress. Cat watched anxiously as it covered fifty,
sixty, seventy-five, and one hundred yards.

"There are too many on her," Chance muttered,
worried. "As soon as she makes it to the entrance, we'll
start shifting some of them to our boat and the . . ."
His words died in his throat.

A huge roller had flooded in as he was speaking.
Carried by a powerful wind, it swamped the longboat,
spinning her about and turning her over, spilling those
aboard her in a tumble of clutching hands and thrashing
legs.

Cat felt as if he had been turned to stone. He
couldn't move. He couldn't close his eyes to the horror, couldn't close his ears to the appalling screams of
the dying.

"Oh dear God!" Bessie Taylor moaned. "When does
it end?"

Chance had sprung up, maddened by the sight,
shouting, "The children. We must get to the children!"

"Sit down, man!" Kell said, sharply. "You'll have us
all in the water with them! We'll row back and rescue
whomever we can."

Both men knew, however, that it was hopeless. One
moment the men, women, and children fought desper-
ately in the rough sea, their cries echoing in the cave.
The next, there was not a sign of life. It was as if they
had never existed. In the dreadful silence that followed, only the shrill wind and the rushing water could
be heard.

"Are they all gone?" Cat whispered, shocked. Who could believe that death could be so swift, so ruthless?

Kell nodded somberly.

"God rest their souls," MacCool O'Shea said huskily.

A kind of paralysis seized those in the quarterboat as they sat staring blankly at the water. Kell roused himself first and said, urgently, "We'd best pull for the entrance. Every moment we linger adds to our own peril."

"We can't just go and leave them here," Cat said, stupefied, still in a daze. Nothing could be done, but his mind could not accept the terrible truth.

"Their troubles are over." Kell had no wish to be unkind or brusque with Cat, but he was concerned now for the fate of the living. "Ours are just beginning," he muttered, almost under his breath, but O'Shea heard.

"Aye," he echoed, "ours *are* just beginning."

"Let's put our backs to it then," Kell went on. The men at the oars rowed with fervor, sending the quarterboat charging through the swirling waters. When they reached the entrance, all of them turned and looked back — one long remembering glance — and then they were through and out in the open.

When they emerged, they were greeted by the three men who had been waiting outside the entrance since the captain had sent them there.

"Cat!" Smithy cried. "Thank God you're safe!"

Cat looked at Smithy with surprise. He and Billy had gotten along well enough on the *Moonraker*, but Billy had never been a special friend. In fact, Cat had found Spencer Gray's company more interesting, for Gray could spin Maori tales that Cat found fascinating.

Willis, his voice rough with emotion, asked, "Is the captain gone?"

Chance nodded. "The captain. The ship. Everything. Everyone."

"We're lucky to be alive," Slush gasped.

Lucky? It was a strange word to describe their condition, Cat thought. He stared about with a grim face at the stretch of empty gray sea, at the sullen sky. The two boats bobbed on the water, seeming to Cat's eyes to shrink to toy size, lost in the vastness of space. Lucky? He supposed it could be called luck, for they had survived, ten out of the eighty-three who had set out from Melbourne such a short time ago. Lucky, because their eyes were still open and their hearts still beating. He recalled the exchange between Kell and O'Shea. He had not quite absorbed at the time what Kell had meant when he had said their troubles were just beginning. Now he felt the weight of Kell's words. Who knew what lay ahead for them now, Cat wondered sadly.

"Mr. Chance," Willis called. "What's our course now?"

"I'd like to transfer to the other boat," Slush said, unexpectedly, before Chance could reply. "They'll need another man at the oars."

"I think the mate should be the one to transfer," Billy objected.

"Smithy's right," Chance agreed. "You can take charge here, Kell. But someone should be in charge of the other boat."

Kell agreed. "But if Slush changes over with you," he added, "one of the other men had better transfer to us. We'll need him at the oars."

"I'll change over," Reid Willis offered.

Gingerly, Willis and Chance exchanged places in the two boats. Then Slush made ready to leave the one quarterboat for the other.

"Wait," Cat said. He gave Slush a defiant look. Maybe this wasn't the right time or the right place, but Cat plunged ahead anyway. "Before you go into the other boat, I want my greenstone jade back."

Slush paused. "You what?" he demanded in disbelief. "Have you gone clean out of your mind? What would I be doing with your fool charm?"

"You took it," Cat persisted. "I felt you take it on the ship."

"Why would I take it?" Slush repeated.

"Because you're superstitious, that's why," Cat flashed back at him. "Because you knew no harm can come to the wearer of the greenstone jade."

"Did you see me take it?" Slush's eyes bored into Cat's. "Aha! Of course you didn't," he snapped, as Cat reluctantly shook his head. "Because I didn't. And I don't like being called a thief. If we were back on the *Moonraker*, I'd show you how much I don't like it, young Cat." He glared, and muttering, made his way carefully into the other boat. "Calling me a thief," he mumbled.

Billy Smithy clutched at his shirt, shivering. "It's so cold," he said. "Can't we get started?"

"Smithy is right," Kell agreed. "This is no time to settle differences. Now we take first things first. As we can all see," he went on, "there's not a chance of a landing hereabouts." His glance, which all followed automatically, took in the cliffs that rose forbiddingly

40

from the churning sea. "Mr. Chance," he called, "do you know these parts? Are we near Disappointment Island?"

"My reckoning is that Disappointment Island lies about six miles off to the north."

"Shall we pull for the island then?"

"You lead, and we'll follow," Chance replied.

"I am so thirsty," Bessie Taylor said suddenly. She had huddled in the boat, her arms folded, shaking with cold, silently listening to the exchange of conversation. "Could I have some water?"

"I should like to oblige you, ma'am, but there is no water," Kell said quietly.

"No water? No water at all?" she repeated Kell's words, aghast.

"Not a drop."

Cat licked his lips. He had not thought of wanting a drink until Mrs. Taylor had asked for water. Now he could feel how irritated his throat and lips had become from the sea. He ran his fingers across his mouth.

"Will there be water on the island?" Cat asked anxiously.

Kell started to shrug his shoulders, thought better of it, and said kindly, "I've no doubt of it at all, lad."

"Well, that's only six miles off," Bessie Taylor said, feeling comforted.

Cat stared at her. Only six miles off! How little Mrs. Taylor knows about the sea, he thought. The wind had risen; the weather was cold and raw even though the sun was struggling to break through the cloud cover. Why there wasn't one among them who was properly dressed for the weather, Cat saw. Some of the seamen wore coarse heavy shirts of wool. O'Shea and Kell and Chance had jackets. And Mrs. Taylor wore a heavy skirt and coat. All of them were soaked through; three of the men had lost their boots in the cavern.

These are probably going to be the longest six miles of our lives, Cat realized. And what, he asked himself miserably, are we going to find at the end of those miles?

"Are we ready then?" Kell shouted across the roar of the wind. At a nod from Chance, Kell added, "Well, follow us and let's put our backs to it."

An hour passed, then two, then three. Again and again the high running breakers spilled over into the quarterboats. Like the others, Cat shivered as the chill wind howled and flung the stinging icy spray in his face. He had often been tired on the *Moonraker*. Now he learned a weariness that seeped through every pore of his body, into the very marrow of his bones.

"Bail, Cat, bail!" That was MacCool O'Shea urging him on each time Cat stopped to rest.

Bail, toss. Bail, toss. Cat moved like a robot; only the dull ache in his arms, hands, and back kept him aware that he was moving. Every now and then, Cat straightened up and looked back to see how those in the other boat were faring. Sometimes he could see them rowing and bailing. Sometimes the boat and the men seemed to disappear completely in the billows.

Cat felt sorry for Bessie Taylor. Her face was drawn, her eyes glazed with fatigue. Yet she didn't complain, but kept steadily at her task — bail and toss, bail and toss.

Cat's glance moved away from Mrs. Taylor's face, moved on, upward, watched sea birds wheeling in the sky. Oh to have wings and fly, Cat dreamed, and voiced his thought aloud.

"To be sure," O'Shea answered lightly. "We'll all be flying up there one day no doubt. When fish can whistle and pigs can dance, most likely."

"Or men can walk on the moon," Willis said gruffly.

Cat didn't feel much like smiling but he couldn't help himself. He had no idea that Willis could come up with such a fanciful notion.

The early morning sun had played games overhead, slipping from behind clouds to send glimmers of brightness shimmering on the water, then hiding for long stretches of time. Cat had started the day by watching the position of the sun in the sky, to judge how much progress the boats were making. After a while, however, he kept his head down, for the sun moved far too slowly across the sky. From the eastern horizon it seemed to come to a standstill directly overhead. Then it disappeared and emerged again, beckoning them westward with a trail of streaming colors that flamed golden fire like a promise. But the promise was false.

After more than twelve hours of steady rowing, they made a bitter discovery. They had not reached an island, but a large formation of rocks, some with needlepoint spires that reached up sharply, as if to pierce the darkening sky.

Cat stared dully at the rocks. No beach. No shore.

Bessie Taylor held back her tears with difficulty. The men looked at Kell as if he was responsible for what they beheld.

"All these hours, breaking our backs, and for what? We're no better off than we were," Billy said hoarsely.

"A whole lot worse, if you ask me," Slush put in sourly. "We're tired and hungry and still at sea."

They had been proceeding northward, intending to move leeward out of the wind for protection. The sea had quietened; the wind had begun to drop.

"Pull head to wind," Kell now commanded, ignoring the complaints. "I can make out a large mass about a mile and a half northeast. It must be Disappointment Island."

"And what if we can't land there either?" Willis asked dubiously.

"Is it a guarantee you're asking?" O'Shea was impatient. "If you've a better idea, then spit it out. If not, then keep your mouth shut."

"Oh, please," Bessie Taylor begged. "What good can all this bickering do?"

It was the bone weariness and the sore ache of their dashed hopes, Cat felt like telling her. He could feel it in himself, bitterness rising in him like a geyser about to spill over. He, too, wanted to snap at Kell, unleash his frustration, blame *somebody* for the situation in which they found themselves now.

Omar Chance settled the matter. "Lead on, Mr. Kell. We'll follow you as before."

The rowing and bailing went on. As the sun dipped in the western sea and vanished, the first boat reached the rock. Twenty minutes later, it was joined by the second quarterboat.

Cat felt a soft touch, then another, on his face. He put his hand to his cheek. Snow! It was snowing!

"It can't be snow," he said surprised. "It's the fourteenth of *May*. It's spring."

"Not here, Cat. It's winter in the Aucklands," Omar Chance reminded him. "You're a long way from Boston. The Auckland Islands are practically on the upper rim of the Antarctic Ocean, did you know that?"

Winter, Cat despaired. At home in Boston, the birds would be singing, the trees would be in full leaf, and the flowers would be bursting with blooms.

"Winter," Cat repeated slowly, and put his hand to his face again.

As the flakes fell more thickly, they stared at one another miserably.

"We'll lie off the island for the night," Kell said, keeping his voice matter-of-fact. "We'll keep on our oars to prevent us from being blown away from the land. In the morning, we'll pull round the north end of the island. We're sure to find a beach or shore there."

"I wish we had water," Bessie said faintly.

"And something to eat," Willis added.

"You'll notice that all the provisions are in your boat," Slush pointed out. "I say we have as much right to it as the others."

"We should save what we have until we get ashore somewhere," Kell cautioned. "We don't know yet what lies ahead."

"We can be dead later, for all we know," Gullitt said angrily. "I say we put something in our bellies now."

"I agree, Mr. Kell," Omar Chance put in unexpectedly. "I think we'd feel better with even a little food under our belts. And I think Mrs. Taylor needs to have something to eat."

"To eat salt meat now will only provoke more thirst," Kell insisted, but seeing that he could change no one's mind, he carefully portioned the same measure of food to all, and as carefully saved the can that had held the meat.

For the remainder of the night, the two boats stayed close to one another, with the men taking their turn at the oars. Those who could closed their eyes and slept in short troubled spurts.

Daylight came creeping slowly across the horizon. In the early dawn, they studied the surface of the rock.

"Can we land, Mr. Kell?" Cat was surveying the rock dubiously.

"We can try. I doubt that we can stay. But we may find some water."

The quarterboat drew closer to the inhospitable shore. O'Shea and Spencer Gray slid into the water, to help pull the boat to land. Their movements, coupled with a sudden swell in the sea, capsized the boat.

Cat sputtered to the surface and looked about. The others were swimming for the shore. Bessie Taylor, helped by Gray, was already there. Both were standing with their bodies hunched against the wind, rubbing their arms in a vain effort to keep warm.

"The provisions!" Kell shouted when he came up, and dove again. Chance and Cat dove with him. They groped in the sullen sea, their eyes stinging from the salt water. Their fingers made contact. Cat came up grasping a piece of pork. Kell and Chance found some cans of meat.

When the party were together again, they discovered that they had lost all the provisions with the exception of the pork Cat had rescued and nine cans of meat.

"That's what comes of letting you keep all the provisions," Gullitt said sullenly. "If we'd had our share aboard our boat, we'd still have at least half the supplies."

Kell did not reply. Instead he suggested they go about the business of finding water. His own throat and lips were sore and parched, his tongue like a heavy dry stick, cleaving to the roof of his mouth. He knew the others suffered from the same symptoms. They had to have water.

Pairing off for the search they fell into natural teams according to their liking for one another. It was not long before Cat and Gray shouted triumphantly, "Water!" The others came racing back at the welcome cry.

Bessie cupped the precious liquid in her hands; Slush fell to the ground and lapped it. No one cared about the manner in which it was done.

"If only we could find some food," Billy said longingly, his thirst satisfied. But a search for food proved hopeless.

"It's plain we'll not survive here on this desolate rock," O'Shea muttered. "There's naught here but water."

"We'll move on, MacCool." Kell called Spencer

Gray to his side. "Would you be knowing anything at all of the Aucklands?"

"Not much," Gray admitted. "There were some Maoris who tried to settle on the Aucklands, but that was at leasty twenty years ago. No, more than that." He tried to recall the date. "About 1842. Maybe 1843. I'm not too sure of the date. But they didn't stay long."

"They might have left some supplies behind, or at least some sort of shelter," Kell said thoughtfully.

Gray seemed doubtful.

Gullitt had come close to listen to the two men. Now he offered a ray of hope.

"I don't know what the Maoris left on the island, but I did read about Captain Musgrave's wreck. A man like that would surely have left supplies behind."

"Was he rescued?" Cat asked eagerly. One by one the others had come and joined Gray and Kell, listening intently to what was being said.

"Captain Musgrave? Not him. Found his own way back to New Zealand," Gullitt said positively.

"The Aucklands are made up of a number of islands. I think we have a better chance of rescue on the main island," Omar Chance said. "Let's get back into the boats and head there."

He turned and led the way back to the boats. The others followed and took their places as before.

Cat stared at the expanse of sea to be covered. Another full day of rowing! Cat felt as if he had been beaten and then, when he could take no more, had been beaten again. Could he endure another exhausting struggle with the hostile sea and wind? He looked at the others. The men were strong — one had to be

strong and rough to live and work on a square-rigger —
but the cold, the wetness, and the hunger had taken
their toll.

Yet now they bent once more, grimly, to the task of
getting the boats across the angry rollers. And as before, it seemed to Cat that the sun, when it was visible,
crawled at a snail's pace across the sky.

They had begun their journey at daybreak. Evening
was blending horizon, water, and sky when Cat suddenly cried out, "Look there! I think I see a bay!"

"Land ho!" Billy Smith shouted. "Land ho!"

They had found safe harbor at last. Securing their
boats on the beach, they staggered ashore, and fell exhausted to the ground.

"This must be Sarah's Bosom," Omar Chance said,
trying to remember what he had read about the Aucklands. "The captain who discovered these islands returned later in a ship called the *Sarah* . . ."

He stopped speaking when O'Shea called out, "Later,
man, later. Have mercy. We need to sleep."

Sarah's Bosom.

Cat, stretched out on the blessed ground that did not
move and rock beneath him, thought it was the most
beautiful name he had ever heard.

6

A Thief Discovered

CAT COULD HEAR the voices before he opened his eyes. He was reluctant to wake up, for as long as he remained caught up in slumber, he could escape the present into his dreams. But the coldness seeped into his body. Strange, that sudden coldness again when he had felt so much warmer during the night. Wide awake now, he sat up to look around. No wonder he felt so cold. During the night, the castaways had huddled against one another, gaining body warmth from each other. But the others had long since arisen; only Cat had been able to sleep on as one by one the others had begun to stir.

"I've always loved the land," O'Shea was saying as Cat joined the others, "but never as much as now!" He was smiling.

"I agree." Bessie Taylor was looking around. "It's a desolate place, but oh, the pleasure of putting one's feet down and walking about."

"We did it." Gullitt's eyes gleamed with satisfaction. "We survived!"

They were all in a much better mood, Cat noticed as he studied his fellow castaways, in spite of the fact that their physical condition had not changed. Their clothes were still damp and clammy; they had no shelter against the winter chill, and their supply of food was meager.

The thought of food started hunger pangs in Cat's stomach. He had heard that if one did not eat for several days, the desire for food was lessened. If so, it was not working in his case. He was ravenous.

"I'm hungry," Cat said baldly.

"I don't think we should touch our provisions until we have searched the island for food and water," Kell advised.

"I'm sure you're right, Mr. Kell," Bessie Taylor agreed, "but I think that if we are to hunt for food, we must have the strength to do so. We must eat something."

"The lady is right," Gullitt said. "We're hungry *now*. I say we eat."

"No. Not yet," Kell insisted. "we've held out this long. We can wait a bit longer." He looked at Bessie Taylor. "Or we can give Mrs. Taylor and Cat a wee bit of food . . ."

"I'll take nothing if the others do not share likewise," Bessie Taylor said evenly. "I want no favors, Mr. Kell. I may not have the physical strength you all have, but I am no weakling." Her eyes were defiant. She stood tall and proud, daring Kell to treat her as less than equal to the others.

Cat stepped to her side. "And I don't like being treated like a child. I've earned the right to be treated like a seaman, just the same as Billy or any of you."

Cat's stomach was grumbling; he worried that the others might hear it growling. But if the others had to wait, then he would wait, too.

"Cat's right," Gullitt said. "We're seamen. We didn't pick you to do our thinking for us, Mister. If anybody talks for us, it's the mate." He turned to Omar Chance. "What do you say, sir? It's up to you."

Chance shook his head. His eyes had a glazed look, and his face was flushed. "We're not seamen and passengers here. In this place, we can only follow the man who can teach us how to survive." He waved his hand at Kell. "We need a resourceful man. I'll stand by any decisions Mr. Kell makes."

All eyes were on Kell, who said slowly, "All right. We'll portion out some food. But mind what I tell you now, decisions have to be made. If we have a debate every time we make a move, we'll go hungry and homeless. I grant you are seamen and on board ship such decisions would be made by the captain or the mate. But we're on land now, and I tell you plain I've roughed it enough to know how to stay alive. And that's why I've put myself in charge. Anyone who wants to challenge that can do so later, but now we gather some of those bracken branches and a bit of the dry grass and build ourselves a fire."

Fire! Cat thought. The word itself was warming to hear. "We can dry our clothes," Cat said with enthusiasm. "And we can cook our food."

"Fire!" Billy said. "What are we waiting for?" He began to scramble around, picking up dry grass and brush.

One by one, the castaways brought what they could find, their faces intent and eager. There was a rush of good feeling among them. Their spirits were lifted, and they smiled as they ran about and then brought what they found, heaping it in a pile until Kell decided they had enough.

Fire. Fire. Fire. The word flickered bright and beautiful in Cat's mind. The flame would blaze; the wood would make a pleasant crackling sound as the fire devoured it.

"Now for a match," Kell said. Every eye was upon him. Willis, a rugged, rough-looking man with a massive jaw, grinned, showing a mouthful of crooked teeth that seemed to have been pitched in at random by some careless hand. Slush rocked back and forth nervously. Each person made some gesture that showed how tense this moment was. Cat rubbed his mouth and bit at his fingers. The match. Hurry, Mr. Kell. Find the match, Cat urged silently.

Kell was searching his pockets, first one, then another. Each time his hands came up empty.

"I know I have matches," he said, puzzled.

"You do. You do," Cat called. "I saw you put them in your pocket. You were smoking your pipe on the *Moonraker*, remember? You had just lit it when Captain Laws called you to help man the quarterboat."

"That's right," Kell said. "When Captain Laws called me, I knocked my pipe against the rail." He felt his pockets. "I must have lost the pipe in the water somehow. But not the matches. Surely never the matches!"

He took his jacket off and searched again. Finally, he flung the jacket from him in frustration.

"Empty your pockets," he urged the men. "It's not possible that one of us . . ." His voice trailed off as one by one the men shook their heads.

They faced each other in dead silence across the useless pile of bracken and dry grass.

"I know how to start a fire without matches," Cat said suddenly. "My brother Ned and I used to do it at home. Indian style. I just need two sticks."

"Out of the mouths of babes," MacCool O'Shea said with hope. "Begging your pardon for the expression," he added hastily, when Cat sent him an angry glance. "Here, laddie, let me help you find your two sticks."

Together they kneeled and dug into the bracken. Cat examined the branches carefully before he finally chose two that felt dry to his hand. He could feel how intently the others were watching his every move, but he felt confident. How often he had done this at home, he and Ned. The memory brought a small smile to his lips as he grated the two sticks against one another.

Rub. Rub. Rub.

Burn! Cat shouted in his mind. Burn! Burn! Burn!

No answering spark flew upward. At last Spencer Gray reached down and took the sticks gently from Cat's hands. Cat remained kneeling, his face turned aside, flushing with the bitterness of his comedown.

Once again, the castaways were in a state of shock. The new disappointment made anger bubble to the surface again.

"So much for Indians," Slush muttered. "Grown men standing about watching a snip of a boy playing with sticks."

"It works," Cat said defensively. "I've done it lots of times."

"Sure it works," Billy yelled. "We just saw how good it works, didn't we?"

"Let him be!" Bessie Taylor flared. "At least he tried."

"Cat is right," Spencer Gray told them. "You can start a fire that way. *Only not with this wood.* This wood is too damp. Sometimes the Maoris of New Zealand still come this way. I remember now that they always bring their own lightwood for their fires."

"The half-breed would know," Gullitt said with contempt.

Cat's nostrils flared with anger. Gullitt had no right to talk that way about Spencer Gray. If I were a man, Cat thought, clenching his hands into tight fists. But he wasn't, and there was nothing he could do, except to shout, "Mr. Gray's worth ten of you!"

Gullitt was about to say something sharp to Cat when Kell said bluntly, "That kind of talk will stop here and now, and we'll be having no more of it. We'll be here a long time, I've no doubt, and our strength lies in each other. You'll be keeping your thoughts to yourself, Mr. Gullitt, or you'll answer to me."

Cat had moved off, still smarting from his failure to strike a spark from the sticks. While Kell was talking, Cat absentmindedly picked up Kell's jacket and began to search through the pockets. Ned, Cat remembered, had always complained how coins kept slipping through tiny openings in the seams of the lining. Cat's fingers probed. Sure enough! There was a small hole in the lining of Mr. Kell's jacket. He tore the lining further, so that he could dig down. His fingers touched something familiar.

"Matches! Mr. Kell. Look! You did have matches.

They just slipped down into the lining," Cat shouted joyfully.

"God bless you for a persistent lad!" O'Shea crowed. "Give them here, Cat, and we'll light them."

Beaming, their good feeling restored again, the castaways watched as Cat gravely handed the matches to John Kell.

"Six matches," Kell marveled. Kneeling, he took one of the matches and drew the head along the surface of a rock. The sound was loud in the watchful silence. In a moment, the scratching ceased.

"It's too damp," Kell said at last. "It won't light."

"You've got five more," O'Shea said urgently. "Light another!"

Again Kell tried the second, the third, the fourth match against the stone — the heads fell off. Now only two matches remained.

"Light them! Light them!" Billy shouted, in a frenzy.

Kell shook his head. "They're too damp," he insisted.

Gloom settled upon the group, heavy as the fog that had imprisoned the *Moonraker*. And then Cat remembered something else Ned had taught him. It would work. It had to work. The castaways would probably make some remark about Indian tricks, but he didn't care.

"Mr. Kell," Cat urged. "Put the matches in your hair and leave them there for a while. They'll dry."

Kell looked at Cat but made no move to do what Cat suggested.

"Please, Mr. Kell," Cat begged. "What harm can it

do? The matches won't light now anyway."

"Give one to Mrs. Taylor and let her tuck it away in her hair," Omar Chance said suddenly.

Wordlessly, Kell handed her one of the two matches. She placed it carefully in her thick hair. Then Kell took the remaining match and put it in his own hair.

"Oh God," O'Shea prayed, looking up. "Dear God. Please let this work."

"While we wait for the matches to dry, I'm going to see if I can find some edible plants," Kell said. "Mac-Cool, you come with me."

Gray offered to go down to the beach. "I noticed some limpets on the rocks. Care to come with me, Cat?" he asked.

"I'll come along, too," Willis said. "I think I can get an albatross. Who knows?" He shrugged his shoulders. "We may even be able to cook it before this day is over."

"No! Not an albatross, Willis!" Slush shrilled. "Don't you know that's bad luck?"

Willis stared at Slush. "Bad luck? *Bad luck?* What do you call what's happened to us so far? Bad luck," he repeated, making a hissing sound from between his gritted teeth as he walked away. "Guess who'll be there for the first bite if I do catch a bloody bird."

Down at the shore, Gray showed Cat how to pluck the limpets from the rocks. The shells covering the small-bodied sea animals reminded Cat of tiny bowls turned upside down. While the shells protected the limpets from sea birds, they could not save them from Cat, who was carefully dislodging them from their tight grip on the rocks.

Further down the shore, a large bird, its wingspread enormous, hovered in the air, then skidded to a stop on the ground. Its large heavy bill looked dangerous and powerful. Its short legs, ending in webbed feet, gave it a curious, awkward walk.

"I'll give Willis a hand," Gray whispered. He moved quickly down the beach to join the other man.

"An albatross isn't turkey," Willis whispered, "but beggars can't be choosers. I think we can catch him if we rush him from both sides."

The albatross objected, uttering a cross between a scream and a groan when it was attacked, and trying to peck first at Willis and then at Gray with its vicious beak. Cat watched the battle with interest, glad he wasn't involved. Pulling the limpets from the rocks, he decided, was far less exhausting.

"I think we have enough for now," Gray said, when the two men returned to Cat's end of the beach, carrying the heavy bird between them. "Let's go back and see what luck the others have had."

They arrived back at the campsite in time to hear Omar Chance talking to the others.

"We've got to get a fire going." Chance's teeth were chattering and he was obviously shivering.

"But Mr. Kell and Mr. O'Shea haven't come back yet," Bessie Taylor objected.

Chance didn't seem to hear her. "Give me the match. We'll start the fire."

She studied Chance, for his manner seemed strange, his eyes too bright. "Are you all right?" she asked, concerned.

"I asked you for the match . . ."

"Mr. Chance, you said Mr. Kell was to make the decisions," Cat said anxiously.

Chance made no answer. He walked toward Mrs. Taylor, holding out his hand, his manner threatening. "The match. Give me the match."

Reluctantly, she dug into her hair and removed the small stick, placing it on Chance's outstretched hand. He felt the match, then passed it from hand to hand, asking each person in turn eagerly if the match was dry enough to light.

"It's dry, isn't it, Cat?"

"Please, Mr. Chance. I can try to find Mr. Kell . . ."

But Omar Chance was already kneeling beside a rock, his hand trembling, staring at the match as if he had forgotten why he had asked for it or what it was. Then, suddenly, he scraped the match along the rock. It lit! The heady smell of sulphur rose in the air as the match burned. Chance was lost in the wonder of the flame.

Cat cried out, "Throw it on the bracken, Mr. Chance. Before the match goes out!" But even as Cat spoke, it was already too late. The flame had traveled along the stick quickly; when it reached Chance's fingers, he dropped the match instinctively. It fell to the ground while Chance stared down at it in a daze.

Reid Willis's face mottled with rage. "I'm going to kill you," he whispered. "I'm going to tear you apart with my bare hands." He started toward Chance but found himself caught and held in a viselike grip.

"Take your hands off me, Gray," Willis roared.

Cat knew how Willis felt; the same sense of shock and

anger was racing through his body. But he was glad, nonetheless, that Gray had kept Willis from harming Mr. Chance. On board the *Moonraker*, under the most trying conditions, the quiet man with the serious eyes had always been in command of himself and others. But now there was something wrong, something very strange about his behavior.

It was into this scene that Kell and O'Shea walked.

"What is it? What's happened?" Kell asked sharply. He listened quietly until he learned that Chance had struck the match and it had lit. For the first time since the shipwreck, Kell lost control of his temper. He strode across the space between himself and Chance and felled the other man with a single blow that laid the mate on the ground. "Where's the fire then, you bloody ape? Where's the fire?"

He's struck the mate! Cat ran to Chance, his eyes filled with anger. He admired Mr. Kell, looked up to him. But Kell had struck the *mate*.

Bessie Taylor moved to Chance's side instantly. She put her hand on his cheeks and then on his forehead.

"The man's ill," she said at last. "He's burning up with fever."

"I'm sorry, ma'am," Kell said, after a moment. "I have no excuse." He looked at Cat as if he could feel Cat's resentment, then looked away. "I apologize to all of you." He walked a slight distance away, approaching a large rock. "We'll do what we can for Mr. Chance in a little while. But our first consideration is still a fire. Cat, I'll thank you to pick up the stumps of the other matches and put them in with the brush pile. They may catch on when we light the fire."

He pulled the last match from his hair and held it loosely between his forefinger and thumb, waiting as Cat scurried about, picking up the broken match heads and sticks and carefully placing them beneath some of the drier twigs. When he was done, Kell made ready to strike the last match.

"Will you bide a moment, Johnnie?" O'Shea called out. "Before you strike the match, I want to kneel and pray." Without waiting to see if his request was granted, he dropped to his knees. "You'll surely not be praying standing up?" he reminded the others quietly, looking from one to the other.

"I'm not a praying man," Willis said roughly, but as slowly, one by one, the others dropped to their knees and bowed their heads, he joined them.

Cat studied his fellow castaways. What a strange mixture of survivors we are, he thought. They had come together to this small island from different parts of the world — from America, from England and Ireland, from New Zealand. They were a hodgepodge of humanity who would have to learn to live with one another more closely than any family.

"Are you not praying?" O'Shea asked sharply.

Cat lowered his head and whispered fervently, not for rescue — that would come later — but for the blessing of fire.

When all were finished with their prayers, they did not rise but stayed as they were while Kell got to his feet and moved off to the closest rock. His eyes raked them one more time before he turned his full attention to the task ahead. The hand holding the match quivered; Cat saw the fingers plainly shaking. Then

Kell pulled the match quickly against the stone.

Bessie Taylor gasped. O'Shea said reverently, "Jesus!" Spencer Gray's eyes seemed to lighten. Slush and Billy whooped with joy. Cat remained frozen, waiting, while Kell, unsmiling and silent, concentrating on keeping the small flame alive, cupped his hand around the flickering light. He touched it to the dry grass in the brush heap, standing back as soon as he had done so, his eyes fixed on the bracken.

Cat became aware of an ache in his thumbs. Looking down at them, he realized that unconsciously he had clasped his hands, pressing one over the other so his thumbs gripped, grasping them harder and harder as he waited for that first telltale wisp of smoke. There it was! A faint spiral of blue gray smoke curled out of the bracken, followed by a small crackling sound.

The castaways grinned at one another. Forgotten were the small animosities, the quick anger, and the hard words. They were alive! They had fire!

As the flames shot up, they hugged one another, pounding each other with unrestrained joy. When they quietened down at last, they drew close to the fire, stretching their hands out to its warmth.

"We can cook the limpets and the albatross now," Billy said happily, and then immediately frowned. "But how are we going to cook them?"

"My brother Ned," Cat suggested, "told me that the Indians used to dig pits in the ground and then they dropped hot stones into the pits. There are plenty of rocks around here. We could try it, anyway."

"Cat is right," Gray agreed at once. "The Maoris also dig a hole in the ground, perhaps two feet deep.

The pit is lined with stones heated on the fire. The meat is placed on the hot rocks, and all of it is covered over with grass and small twigs. Then soil is shoveled in over it all. The flesh of some animals is well cooked in about two hours."

"That's all very well," Bessie Taylor said quietly, "but we've no shovels to dig pits with."

"True," O'Shea agreed, "but we have the cans from the meat we ate. You saved those two cans, didn't you, Johnnie?" He grinned when Kell nodded. "You'll find," he added gleefully, "that Johnnie is a saving man, the Lord be blessed."

Humming tunelessly, almost as if he were back in the galley on the *Moonraker*, Slush set about preparing the first meal the castaways had eaten in almost three days. No one left the fire. All were still weary and cold. The sight of the seafood and the bird cooking in the improvised pots made their mouths water.

Omar Chance, lying on an improvised bed of bracken covered with dry grass, stirred restlessly. He had fallen into a feverish sleep. Looking down at him, Cat wondered how the mate could be fed some of the broth from the pot. If this wasn't practical, then maybe Mr. Chance could eat bits of the cooked limpets. He needed food. They all needed food.

Cat was relieved to see that Willis woke the mate, holding him up almost to a sitting position, and that Mr. Chance was able to swallow some of the food.

"You're a fine cook," Bessie Taylor told Slush generously, a compliment Slush accepted as his due.

The others agreed with Bessie. Neither Slush nor the rest of the castaways, Cat noticed with interest, remembered how they had hated Slush's cooking aboard the *Moonraker*. Cat sank his teeth into the meat of the bird. Maybe, he reflected, Slush's cooking hadn't been all that bad.

When the meal was over, Kell suggested that they think of preparing some shelter against the coming of night. Bessie Taylor, however, had another suggestion.

"I think, Mr. Kell, that had better wait a bit. Mr. Chance's clothes are still quite damp. I think the men had better remove their shirts and dry them completely before the fire."

"No, ma'am," Willis protested immediately. "Not in your presence."

"We cannot stand upon ceremony here, Mr. Willis. We already have one sick man on our hands. Billy has been sneezing steadily. Cat is beginning to cough. We shall be very lucky if we do not all come down with colds or worse."

"It won't help to take our shirts off," Billy insisted. "It's freezing. The fire can't keep us warm enough."

"It could," Cat said, thinking aloud, "if we built another pile of bracken and lit it. We could stand between the two bonfires and be warm back and front at the same time," he finished triumphantly.

"A splendid idea," Bessie Taylor agreed. Some of the men scattered again to pick up brush and grass. Others improvised drying racks out of branches for their damp clothing.

It will be good to be in warm dry clothes again, Cat thought as the second fire was started. It seemed to him that the temperature was dropping steadily. He was glad to remove his clammy damp shirt and noticed the other men were grateful to be hanging their clothing on the racks. Only Billy Smith for some reason stood aside, watching them with smoldering eyes.

"Here now, Billy," O'Shea called. "You'll not be putting the rest of us to shame. Off with your shirt, and I'll hang it handy to the fire."

Billy backed off. "Leave me alone," he said resentfully. "Just leave me alone."

Cat regarded Billy thoughtfully. What was Billy up to? It couldn't matter that much, could it, just to take off his shirt? It didn't make any sense at all.

"It's all right, Billy," Kell said. "Let the matter drop," he told the others brusquely. "His clothes will dry sooner or later."

Relieved, Billy came back to stand between the two fires. Gullitt, however, was not content to let the matter rest. He stole up quietly behind Billy. Without warning, he reached over and yanked the shirt up and over Billy's head.

"So that's the way of it," Kell said coldly.

Cat gasped. "It was you! And all the time I thought it was Slush!"

"I didn't want to die," Billy shouted at him. "Can't you understand? I didn't want to die."

Gullitt glared. "Save me from a man who steals from his own shipmate." Billy's face grew red under the contempt in Gullitt's voice.

His hands flew to his chest. There, suspended on its seven strings of braided grass, was Cat's greenstone jade.

The thief had been discovered.

7

Blow the Man Down

SURVIVAL! That's the grim task ahead of us now,"
Kell said to the others as they huddled close to the fires.

Billy had taken his place between Willis and Slush,
putting as much space as possible between himself and
Cat, to whom he had reluctantly returned the greenstone jade. Cat's eyes had been hard and unforgiving.
No wonder Billy had cried "Thank God you're safe,"
when Cat and the others had rowed out of the cavern in
the quarterboat. How his conscience must have both-
ered him! And well it should have, Cat brooded. Gullitt was right. To steal from a shipmate *was* un-
forgivable.

Cat didn't like Gullitt any more now than he had on
the ship. And he knew that Gullitt still disliked him,
had not forgotten what he considered Cat's rebel-
liousness on the *Moonraker*. But mean and hard as Gullitt was and could be, he would never have taken the
greenstone jade away from Cat.

Cat sighed. What a mixed-up group they were.

O'Shea was leaning toward Cat, whispering something in his ear.

"What?" Cat asked, startled out of his reverie.

"I said don't be too hard on yon Billy," O'Shea repeated. "When a man feels frightened and cornered,
there's no telling what he'll be driven to do."

Cat let his eyes wander to Billy's face and on to the faces of the others, while his mind considered O'Shea's words. No telling what frightened, cornered men would do. Then what strange and terrible things might still surface as they all faced life together on this bleak and forsaken island? How were they to survive, Cat asked himself darkly.

O'Shea was still talking, but this time he was answering Kell's comment about surviving. He said, with a bright look in his eyes, "My dear sainted mother used to say, 'MacCool,' she'd say, 'hope is a better companion than fear, lad. That and hard work and faith . . . that's all you need to survive in this world.' And I'm a man for hoping and praying, I'll grant you that," he ended with a laugh.

"Agreed," Kell replied instantly. "To sit idly and worry about one's fate wastes a man's energy. There's much we can do and will do whilst we are here . . ."

"Whilst we are here." Willis picked up Kell's words. "Do you mean you think there's a chance we may be rescued?"

"Why not?" Kell asked reasonably. "Can we not hope, as O'Shea suggests? But against that day, we will help ourselves." He turned to Gullitt, who was sitting and staring pensively at the flames. "Mr. Gullitt, you spoke of Musgrave's wreck some time back. Refresh my memory, for I've no recollection of the wreck at all."

"Gray probably knows as much about it as I do," Gullitt began. "I think it was some two or three years ago that Captain Musgrave's ship, I can't remember the name . . ."

"The *Grafton*," Spencer Gray said quietly.

". . . the *Grafton*. Right. She was wrecked somewhere on this or one of the other of the Aucklands, and he and the men of his crew who survived built a fine hut, using the spars and the boards from the wrecked ship."

"They made a thatched roof for the hut with this long tussock grass," Gray took up the story. He pointed to some clumps of tall coarse grass growing in dense stout tufts nearby.

Cat, following the direction of Gray's finger, saw a tangle of grass and scrub strange to his eyes. Back home in Boston, the grass was soft and green. But then, everything he had seen thus far on the island was different from anything he had ever known.

"In the account I read," Gullitt went on, "it seems that Captain Musgrave and his men managed to save some of their stores, too. It could be that they left behind some mighty handy items."

"God knows we need anything we can put our hands on," O'Shea said fervently.

"Amen to that," Willis agreed.

Gullitt spat into the fire. "Now all we have to do," he suggested grimly, "is to find the hut."

Cat jumped eagerly to his feet.

"Why don't we start searching for it now?" he asked. Warmed by the fire, somewhat rested, his belly satisfied, Cat was ready to move on.

"Not so fast," Willis growled. "We're not ready to take to the boats again. Why, we're barely dry. Maybe you've a taste for getting soaking wet again, but I'm not breaking my back at the oars for a while yet."

"But Mr. Willis," Cat began to protest.

"I want no buts from you," Willis snapped. "If I was thirteen, I guess I'd be hopping off six ways to Sunday, too. But I'm not thirteen. I'm sixty . . ." He broke off.

"Sixty!" Slush said, amazed. "You told us you were only forty . . ."

"You're an old man," Gullitt muttered. "A woman, a boy, and an old man on our hands!"

"You'll not live to see the day that you find me dependent upon you, Mr. Gullitt." Bessie Taylor was outraged. "On your hands indeed! I took care of myself after my husband died in Melbourne, and I'll be taking care of myself now, thank you very much!"

"I've worked side by side with you on the *Moonraker* and more than carried my share," Willis reminded Gullitt. "And I'll outwork you here, you can count on that. So don't you old man me!"

Angry words trembled on Cat's lips as well, but Kell interrupted.

"Mr. Willis is right. We need to build our strength. And we must put first things first. What we need is food and shelter. Temporary shelter," he added, as Cat was about to speak. "Mr. Gray can probably show us how to build . . . what do the Maoris call them, Mr. Gray?"

"*Mai-mai.* They are rough shelters built from brushwood and thatched with grass. They are closed in on three sides. My people build a fire in front of the open side. The *mai-mai* keep the cold out fairly well."

But that was what the pioneers in America did, Cat thought with amazement. Ned had described what he had called the "half-face camp." It, too, had three sides, fashioned out of poles and brush. The fourth side, Ned had said, was sometimes covered with the skin of an animal to keep out the wind and the rain. A fire was built in front for warmth and for cooking. How strange that people thousands of miles apart should build the same kind of shelter! He must tell Ned . . . would he ever see Ned again? The thought that he might never see his brother again brought a lump to his throat.

Survival, Cat was beginning to realize, did not mean rescue. It meant just staying alive, and that was all.

He must keep his mind from wandering, Cat told himself sternly, because an argument had begun and Cat had not heard its beginning.

Gullitt was talking, his black eyes brilliant in the glow of the fire, his thin lips drawn back in anger. "I say we vote. Maybe some of us would like to have some voice in what's to be done or not to be done."

"And I say" — Kell stood up, his own eyes beginning to blaze — "that no one eats who doesn't do his fair share of hunting for food. If it's hungry bellies you're after, then take the boats and welcome."

Gullitt backed down. "All right, Kell. I'll go along with you." He paused, then added significantly, "For now."

Kell ignored the threat in Gullitt's words. "It might be a good idea for us to pair off and head in different directions. It will give us some notion of the lay of the land and what we can expect to find hereafter. Mrs. Taylor, I'd take it kindly if you stayed behind and

looked after the mate. And we'll be setting up sched-
ules for duties," he went on, already planning ahead.
"Someone needs to tend the fire, and someone needs to
do the cooking. We'll be sharing that chore. This first
week, Slush, you'll be in charge of both."

Characteristically, Kell did not wait for an answer,
taking it for granted that his suggestions would be carried out as if they had been issued as orders.

Cat hurried off after Kell and O'Shea for he had
questions he was bursting to ask.

"Mr. Kell," he began, puzzled. "I don't understand.
Mr. Gullitt, I mean. And Billy. Mr. Gullitt was ready
to kill Mr. Gray, back on the *Moonraker*. But then he
got mad at Billy for stealing my greenstone jade. It
doesn't make sense to me. I mean . . ."

Kell interrupted. "Now who can understand the
quirks in a man's mind?" he asked. "Our Mr. Gullitt
has a quick temper. He's a man who would kill in the
heat of rage in a fight. But he would not deliberately
steal from a fellow shipmate. Young Billy would be
more likely to back down or run away, or steal, if he's
pushed to it by fear. We're all of us a mixed bag of
feelings and reactions, Cat. I knew a man once who
could have passed for the devil himself. Yet he once
jumped into a river to save a drowning mongrel of a
dog. There's light and the dark of the moon in all of
us . . ."

Cat drew a deep breath. "It's so complicated," he
complained.

"That it is," O'Shea agreed sympathetically. "That
it is." He turned to Kell. "Would it not be a good

idea, Johnnie," he asked, "to have piles of brush and wood at a high point on the island ready to be burned if we sight a ship?"

Cat's eyes lit up. "Do you think a ship might come by?"

Kell considered his reply carefully. "Aye," he agreed at length. "It could happen. And so we'll have a woodpile ready. Maybe several." Seeing how Cat's face grew eager, he cautioned, "But, mind now, it's not likely a ship would be traveling so far from the sea lanes."

"You're overly harsh with the boy, Johnnie," O'Shea objected.

"Not so harsh as the life we'll be leading, MacCool. And I'll not be having Cat dreaming of sails coming up over the horizon when he should be at some chore or other. Nor any of us pinning our hope on rescue."

"You mean we may never get off the island?" Cat asked, his face troubled.

"We shall get off this island, one way or another," Kell replied. "MacCool can tell you I'm not one to give up without a fight. But that day may well be distant, Cat, and we'll all be the better for learning to live with the here and now of it, for it will be a fight every inch of the way, you can count on that." He put his hand on Cat's shoulder. "It's a man you are now, Cat. And it's man to man that I'm telling you the truth as I see it. Are you up to it, then?"

"I'm up to it," Cat said steadily. He followed behind the two men, busy with his thoughts. Then he rushed to catch up with them. "Will we look for Musgrave's hut? After we've finished hunting, I mean."

Kell smiled briefly. "We've no choice but to look. The weather grows colder by the minute. Our clothing is near in tatters. We've need of shelter, Cat, desperate need. Yes, you can depend upon it. We'll be looking for Captain Musgrave's hut soon enough. But the finding of it . . . now that may take some doing."

While they walked and talked, they kept their eyes open for game. Kell and O'Shea fell into a conversation about their young days, growing up in Ireland. While they reminisced, Cat's mind hopped from one thought to another. Slush had carried on about the killing of the albatross — the gooney bird, Slush had called it — but he had eaten it as eagerly as anyone else. Then John Kell had insisted that they save the bird's bones. Nothing must go to waste, he had warned them. Marooned as they were, everything must be put to some use. What good, Cat pondered, were the bones of an albatross?

As they had walked, their steps had taken them toward the beach. Suddenly, O'Shea stopped dead. He caught Cat's arm and said softly, "Whisht now!" He pointed. Below them, lying outstretched upon a flat rock, its large paddlelike flippers twitching, a seal was taking advantage of the wintry sun. It was a huge animal, its fur sleek and shining. As they stared at it with growing excitement, the seal adjusted its heavy body to a more comfortable position.

"Will you look at the darling creature?" O'Shea whispered, grinning. Then, quickly, his mood changed. "And how are we to kill him then?" he asked glumly. "Do we shoot him?" He squinted his eyes and pointed his finger like a gun. "Or use our bows and arrows?"

73

Kell studied the seal, at peace on the rock, unaware of its danger. "Look about, man," he said finally. "Put your hands on the stoutest stick you can find. If we've no weapons, we'll use our hands and beat him to death if we must."

They scattered, peering at the ground. At last they met again, each holding short, thick clublike sticks.

"Heroes to the battle," O'Shea chuckled, waving his club in the air. "And maybe when he sees us and our weapons, he'll oblige us by laughing himself to death."

Cat grinned as they stole quietly down to the beach. The seal, slumbering peacefully, did not stir even when the three hunters approached quite close. But as Cat raised his stick, the seal opened its large black eyes. It seemed to Cat that the animal's eyes bored into his own. At that precise moment, Kell and O'Shea brought their clubs down upon the seal. Sickened, Cat dropped his club. He had never harmed an animal in his life. He could not raise his hand against one now.

"Cat!" O'Shea cried. "Raise your club, lad."

"I can't," Cat said faintly.

"This is no time to come all over squeamish," O'Shea protested. "Damn it all, we need . . ."

"Leave off, MacCool! We've more urgent matters at hand. Quick, man," he shouted, for the seal was preparing to leave the rock and return to the safety of the sea.

Cat had already begun to move away blindly, not caring in which direction his feet took him, his mind in a turmoil. He had failed John Kell, and if Kell was angry, he had every right to be, Cat told himself miserably. Everyone had to pull his weight on the island,

Cat no less than the others. Hadn't Kell just finished telling Cat he was a man? Was this how a man acted?

I don't care, Cat muttered rebelliously, I won't kill. The expression in the eyes of the seal remained with him as he cast himself down upon a rock and stared out across the sea.

Was ever a world so gray, he asked himself wretchedly. Gray sea, and the endless stretch of restless, churning water, rushing off to join a dull slate horizon. Overhead, in the leaden sky, even the wheeling birds were gray. Cat recognized the birds — they were petrels. Slush had told him once that it was bad luck to kill a petrel, adding darkly that each one of the creatures held the soul of a sailor lost at sea.

As Cat stared at the birds now, they dipped and wheeled away, their cries filling the air with a harsh shrill twittering. Cat wondered if a storm was brewing. Storms always followed the sighting of a petrel, sailors believed. And if there was a storm, Cat worried suddenly, how would they keep the fires going?

"It's a heavy burden of woe that sits upon your shoulders I'm thinking," came O'Shea's voice. He had come seeking Cat, still angry at his desertion, but seeing how Cat sat, crushed and still, his face bleak as the sea itself, his anger left. He put his hand on Cat's shoulder, patting him gently, then sat down beside him on the rock.

"You know, Cat," he said after a moment, "there's much we have to do in this life that's not to our liking. But we eat or we die, don't you see. And if it comes to that, laddie, it's not much of a choice we have, is it?"

Cat rose. "I know, Mr. O'Shea. And I'm sorry."

O'Shea raised his hand. "We did what needed doing, Johnnie and I, but now we'll be needing help. Will you be off now and fetch some of the others. If only we had some knives . . ." His voice trailed off, but in a moment he said briskly, "And if wishes were horses, beggars would ride, eh, Cat? Off with you then."

Back at the campsite, Cat found that all but Gullitt and Willis had already returned, some with birds' eggs, Billy with limpets. Gray was busy stockpiling wood for the fire. Omar Chance still lay on his bed of bracken. He seemed more relaxed, his glance following the men as they moved about. He had slept, Mrs. Taylor told Cat with satisfaction, and had only just awakened. The fever, she announced, was dropping rapidly.

The men, cheered by Cat's news about the seal, set out willingly behind him. Billy, rushing ahead to keep stride with Cat, made several attempts to speak to Cat but broke off each time. At last he could take Cat's silence no longer.

"Look here, Cat. You and I were always friends on the *Moonraker*. I know I did a mean, cruel thing, stealing your jade. But I was scared. Can't you understand that? Haven't you ever been scared? Haven't you ever done anything you were sorry for later, when you had time to think about it?" Billy's eyes were large and earnest.

"It's all right, Billy," Cat answered at last. "I was angry . . . I've never had anything like the greenstone jade before. It's something special to me. It's more than good luck . . . I don't know how to say it . . ."
It was the legend, and the gift; it was the friendship and

the heart of the man who gave it. "Never mind, Billy. Now that I have it back, I'm not going to hold your stealing it against you anymore."

Billy hesitated, then said uncertainly, "Would you let me touch it once in a while, just for luck?"

"As long as you never try to take it away again," Cat agreed.

Billy Smithy sighed with relief.

"You don't know what that means to me."

Their attention was attracted by O'Shea calling, "Over here." When they gathered where Kell and O'Shea waited, they were stunned by the size of the seal.

Billy was the first to speak. "How do we get him back?" he asked, puzzled.

"We don't," Kell answered briefly. "We cut him up here."

"What with?"

"We've a need for sharp-edged stones," Kell told them. "I've already found two . . ." He held the stones out for inspection. The men scattered, searching the ground with care, picking up stones and testing them for cutting edges.

Kell had kept Cat at his side. "Will you help with the carving?" he asked quietly, holding out one of the stones.

Cat stood still, his eyes on the stone, his hands limp at his side. · Kell let the silence between them deepen. At last, reluctantly, Cat reached over and took the stone from Kell's hand.

"What do I do first?" Cat asked, in a faint voice.

"We must be careful cutting the hide," Kell explained. "If our luck holds and we capture other seals, we'll have warm clothes for our backs from the hides. Not to mention meat as a change in diet from fish and birds. We can get oil from the blubber." As he talked, Kell was working on the seal, using the sharp-edged stone like a knife. "It may be that I can fashion some oil lamps, if I can find some sort of container."

As the men came back, bearing their stones, Kell cautioned them too about trying to avoid damaging the hide. Cat, fighting down the sick feeling that rose in his throat, accepted finally the stern necessity that he had no choice: It was either the life of the animal or their own lives.

Beside him, O'Shea began to hum as his stone cut away at the seal. Then he sang the words aloud, very softly at first.

> As I was a'walkin' down Paradise Street,
> To me, aye, aye, blow the man down!

Absent-mindedly, Kell blended his voice with O'Shea's.

> A saucy policeman I chanced for to meet,
> Blow the man down, to me, aye, aye,
> Blow the man down.

Cat, feeling suddenly better, joined in the singing.

> Whether he's white man or black man or brown,
> Give me some time to blow the man down.

Absorbed in their work, they all now picked up the sea chantey. For the first time since they had left the *Moonraker*, they had a real sense of comradeship, of sharing, a feeling of working together in harmony for a common cause. This spirit remained with them when they returned to the campsite, carrying chunks of seal flesh and the seal's hide.

"Meat!" Bessie Taylor greeted them happily. "Now if only we had something to season it with . . . a wee bit of salt," she added wistfully.

"Salt," Kell repeated.

"Oh, we have salt," Cat said airily, "but it's all out there, in the sea." He waved his hand toward the beach.

"Exactly so," Kell said, his manner thoughtful. "Cat is right. We do have salt. All we need to do now is find some way of getting it from there," he waved his hand just as Cat had done seconds before, "to our table. In a manner of speaking, of course."

Omar Chance called from his bed, "Evaporation."

Kell turned, surprised. "Are you feeling better then?" he asked, going to greet Chance.

"Food, rest, and warmth can do wonders for the body," Bessie Taylor announced. "His fever is dropping. I think Mr. Chance will be fine very soon."

"Evaporation," Chance repeated.

"We need a pot . . . with the fire going and water in the pot boiling over it. You're right, Mr. Chance. Evaporation would do the rest. The trouble is, we don't have a pot to spare."

"We have the cans with the preserved meat," Cat began, but Kell shook his head firmly.

"We'll not be touching that food. Those cans are our emergency rations. Never mind, lad," he said, seeing how Cat's face fell. "It was a good idea. Perhaps when we start our search for Musgrave's camp, we'll be lucky enough to find some utensils . . ."

He broke off as Gullitt and Willis came bursting back to the campsite, running and shouting.

"We've found a hut," Gullitt shouted triumphantly.

"The walls have fallen in, and the roof is sitting on the rafters, but we could fix it up," Willis said, smiling broadly.

"At least we'll have shelter from the cold. I think we ought to move the fire there," Gullitt said. "It's only about three miles along, on the south side of the bay. We may even find some other abandoned huts around there."

"It's too late now," Kell decided. "But tomorrow, bright and early, we'll make our move."

They grinned at one another. Things were looking up. They had fire, water, and food. If their luck held out, they might be able to make some warm clothing and find shelter against the winter's biting frost. And the mate was obviously better, taking note of everything that was being said and done.

It was into this contented scene that Slush came stumbling in, his face ashen, his legs trembling so that he would have fallen if Spencer Gray had not caught him.

"What is it, man?" Kell asked sharply.

Slush ran his tongue over his lips.

"A ghost!" he shrilled. "There's a ghost on the island!"

And with these words, he fainted dead away.

8

Dead Man's Gold

IT HAD BEEN a strange day. It had begun almost as soon as Kell, determined to find Musgrave's hut, had sailed off in one of the boats, taking with him O'Shea, Gullitt, Billy, and Willis.

Chance, as soon as the men and the boat were out of sight, had assigned those who had remained behind the usual tasks. Since it was Chance's week to do the cooking and tend the fire, it fell to the others to do the hunting — for food, for bracken as a stockpile — and the other daily chores that had become almost routine.

Cat was sent to look for birds' eggs. He was about to depart on this errand when he noticed Slush glancing about and then sneaking off toward the beach. Curious, Cat followed, taking care that Slush did not see him. Slush headed directly toward the beach openly now, positive he had not been seen. Cat, behind him, had to flee suddenly into the underbrush and take cover, for Slush halted, seeming to study the lay of the land, then moved on to where three rocks stood almost in an exact line.

From his hiding place, Cat watched intently as Slush, using the rocks as a guide line, walked directly away from them, counting as he walked.

"One, two, three, four . . ." The count stopped at twenty. Slush paused, gazed about, shook his head, and counted again. "Twenty-one, twenty-two, twenty-three . . ."

Cat was puzzled. What kind of a game was Slush playing?

". . . thirty." Now Slush seemed satisfied. He turned where he stood, scanning the area all about, his eyes lingering and then moving over the bush where Cat froze, holding his breath, so that no little movement might betray him. Then Slush did a curious thing. Tugging at his pants, he forced the material up as high as it would go. There, strapped well above the knee on each leg, were two small wide belts. After a moment's struggle, the belts were loosened and fell to the ground. Slush rubbed his legs, talking to himself, softly, so softly that Cat could not hear what he said.

Now Slush took a rock and began to dig a hole in the ground. It was hard, slow work but Slush was persistent. When the hole was deep enough, he dropped the belts into it, and immediately set to work covering the hole, smoothing the ground when he was finished so that it did not look as if it had been disturbed.

At last Slush stood, stretched, and laughed. Then he counted off one hundred feet additional until he came to a tree. Using a rock, Slush made a notch in the bark. Once more he turned and studied the scene all about. Still laughing, he walked away.

What was it Slush had buried? Cat went and stood at the three rocks, as Slush had done, then counted off thirty paces. He stood and stared down at the ground. I wonder what's there, he asked himself. He wanted to dig it up, look at whatever it was, then bury it again. No, he thought, whatever it is, it's Slush's secret, and

I've no right . . . on the other hand, his mind said persuasively, it might be something that affects the castaways. Then wasn't it their right to know?

Cat was undecided while different thoughts whirled around and around in his brain. Twice he walked away, and twice he came back.

Finally, curiosity winning out, he picked up a sharp-edged rock and began to dig. He found it, as Slush had, tedious and difficult but he kept at it. There! The belts were finally uncovered. Cat picked one up, brushing it free of dirt. It was made of leather and divided into pouches. And there was a name on the belt — Tom Warthy. Tom Warthy? Cat's brow wrinkled. Who was Tom Warthy?

As he puzzled over the name, the man's face suddenly clicked into Cat's mind's eye. Mr. Warthy was the miner with the face like a jigsaw puzzle, the wrinkles in his face running in jagged lines, dividing his face up into small skin areas that looked as if they had been fitted together loosely. Tom Warthy had been hit by one of the falling rocks that had rained down on the *Moonraker*. He had been among the first to die.

Cautiously, Cat peered into the belt. Gold nuggets glittered back at him as the sun touched them. Cat drew a deep breath. This was Tom Warthy's gold. Cat remembered now hearing the miners talk. Tom Warthy had laughed at those who had insured their gold. Tom was too smart for that, he'd said, and slapped his thighs. He'd had two leather belts made for him special, he'd bragged. And his gold was as close to him as his own skin. Heavy? No, sir! That was a sweet weight!

A hand reached down and yanked at Cat's hair. His head was pulled up so that his eyes were within inches of Slush's contorted face.

"Spying!" Slush said, his voice hoarse with rage. "I knew it! I could feel your spying eyes." He held a large rock in his hands. Cat was so frightened he could scarcely breathe. His scalp smarted with pain as Slush's hand tightened on his hair. Slush looked half-crazed. "I ought to kill you. That's what I ought to do. Kill you." He raised the rock.

Cat waited, his heart palpitating, expecting to feel the weight of the rock on his head, knowing that he was within inches of dying. The sunlight, touching the gold again, distracted Slush. He dropped the rock, and suddenly words were spilling from him eagerly.

"You don't know what it's like, Cat. Nobody's ever known. I've been a cook twenty years, Cat. Twenty years! And I've hated every minute of it. In twenty years, I never had a name, did you know that? Slush. Every cook on board ship is called Slush. Or Doc. Like we never had any real names of our own. Well I have a real name. You never heard it, did you, Cat? Hubert Lempert Jones. Hubert — Lempert — Jones."

Cat straightened up warily, although he still remained kneeling. "Why did you go on? Being a cook, I mean, if you hated it so much?"

I'm safe, Cat thought, if I can keep Slush talking.

"What else was I fit for?" Slush asked bitterly. "What else did I know to do? But this gold, see, it makes things different. I can be somebody; when we're rescued and I go back to England, I won't be Slush any more. I won't be Slush ever again. You think I did wrong, don't you," he hurried on, without giving Cat a chance to reply. "Taking a dead man's gold. But it was no use to poor old Warthy, now was it? And if I hadn't taken it, it would just be lying down in Davy Jones's locker, along with Warthy and those other poor souls. You shouldn't look down your nose at me, Cat."

"Oh Slush, I'm not. Why would I?" Cat protested. "Anyway, it's no business of mine, is it? I had no right to follow you and dig this up. And I'm sorry. I'm really sorry, Slush. Would you rather that I called you Mr. Jones from now on?" he added. "Seeing how you feel about being called Slush?"

"Slush I am and Slush I'll be until I set foot again in England. No, Cat. But I'm asking you not to betray my secret. I don't want to have to threaten you, Cat. But I will if I have to."

"You don't have to worry. I wouldn't ever tell. You know that, Slush, don't you?" Cat asked earnestly. "I wouldn't ever tell."

Slush nodded, his mouth dry. "Help me bury it, Cat. Two pair of hands are faster than one."

When they were finished, Cat stood up. "I'm supposed to be looking for birds' eggs."

"And I'm supposed to be helping Spencer Gray start work on building another hut."

Slush started to walk away and stopped. "The weather's changing." A small shudder passed through him. "I feel, I don't know, queerlike."

"It's the sun. It's only gone behind a cloud," Cat said reassuringly. He, too, shivered. He wondered if they would ever be warm again.

Slush and Cat did not speak to one another again all that day, and very little to the others. A strange feeling seemed to come over everyone, all except Bessie Taylor, who went about her tasks quietly and efficiently.

The next day fog rolled in, thick and suffocating. Even to walk a few steps was to lose one's sense of direction. The following day it rained, a freezing Arctic downpour that drove them to huddle together in the hut for protection from the wet and numbing cold.

Bessie Taylor worried about the fire. She urged Chance to bring it indoors, using an empty can as a container for the life-giving flame. It served to keep the hut moderately warm, but when they opened the door to get rid of the smoke, winter crowded in and lived with them.

One by one they fell ill and lay about in the hut, with no interest in eating and barely the strength to move. Only Bessie Taylor still remained untouched by the illness that struck down her companions. Cat watched, his eyes clouded, struggling to understand, as each day Bessie Taylor left the hut, braving the penetrating cold, to hunt unsuccessfully for birds' eggs, but managing to bring back enough limpets to feed them, urging, coaxing, wheedling, and threatening them to get some food into their stomachs.

Time was seen through the narrow haze of sickness. The days came and went. And then, one morning, Bessie Taylor shook Cat gently and said softly in his ear, "They're back, Cat. Mr. Kell and Mr. O'Shea and the others. They're back!"

"Do you think they found Musgrave's camp?" he asked faintly, his voice hoarse and raw. Bessie Taylor had fed them but neither Cat nor the others had been able to keep the food down. The smell of their vomit was sour and strong in the hut. While he had been sick, Cat had not been aware of it. Now that he was somewhat better, he was repelled by the odor.

Cat struggled to sit up. He was rocked by dizziness and clutched at Mrs. Taylor until his head steadied and his vision cleared again.

"How long has it been?" he asked.

"They left about the twenty-first of May," she calculated. "It's the end of June. Five weeks, Cat. Five long, worrisome weeks."

Had they found Musgrave's camp then? Five weeks! They must have found it. Gullitt had said — how long ago it seemed now — that Musgrave and his men had built sturdy huts from the spars and boards of the wrecked ship. There would be tools there, maybe even tins of food.

"I hope you're right," Mrs. Taylor said.

Cat looked surprised. He hadn't realized that he was voicing his thoughts aloud.

Another thought occurred to him. Five weeks. How did Mrs. Taylor know how much time had passed? How could she pinpoint the date so accurately? As if she could read his mind, she said, "Do you remember, Cat, the first day we came to the island? Mr. Kell scratched the date on that large rock on the beach. Each day he made another mark. He said it was our calendar stone. While Mr. Kell and the others were gone, I made a mark each day."

"Why?" What difference did time make here, Cat wondered moodily, when one day passed like the other, and no day had any special meaning.

"I don't know if I can explain," she said, her brow wrinkling as she looked for words that would tell Cat how important this was to her. "Birds, now. How do they know when it is time to fly south? Inside," she pressed her hand to her chest, "instinct tells them it is time to go. People don't have that feeling built into them. They need clocks and calendars. How can we look for spring and summer if we don't know the month of the year? In this weather, we might come to believe that winter will last forever. But each day when I made a new scratch, I thought, one day less of winter, one day closer to spring.

Cat was on his feet now, leaning against Mrs. Taylor as she helped him walk down toward the beach. Chance, Gray, and Slush had already dragged themselves there to greet Kell and the others.

"We're a fine looking crew," Kell said soberly, his glance sweeping over the castaways when they were all assembled, eager for news.

For the first time since his illness, Cat took a good look at the others. "Why, we look like skeletons!" He was stunned. "Do I look like that, too?"

"Well, we've all lost weight," Bessie reminded him. "Me less than you, no doubt." But this was not true. Bessie Taylor's gaunt face and thinness of body told of the toll the past weeks had taken. "Was your trip all that you hoped, Mr. Kell?" She was glad to change the subject.

"Yes. And no!" It was a puzzling reply.

She was about to question Kell further, but Gullitt broke in. "The rain and the wind and the fog! You wouldn't believe the foul weather we ran into. Twice we had to put back in the same bay. We were sick as dogs."

"We found a seal, killed it, and then couldn't swallow as much as a mouthful," Willis muttered. Cat, studying Willis, was startled at the change that had come over the man. On board the *Moonraker*, Willis had seemed to Cat to be like the other seamen — strong, tireless, hardworking. Now illness seemed to have made Willis's body shrink. His face was lined, and he looked worn.

"There were times we felt so sick we could hardly lift our oars out of the water," Billy complained.

"Still," O'Shea noted, his glance moving from face to face, pausing at last to linger thoughtfully on Bessie Taylor, "we seem to be in better shape than you, thanks be to Johnnie here. Forced us to eat seal blubber, he did. Nasty stuff."

Cat's lips curled in distaste at the idea.

"No need to be turning up your nose, laddie," O'Shea said warmly. "We thought we'd not make it back, we were that sick. And then, when we began to eat the blubber, our strength returned."

"Then we shall eat blubber," Bessie Taylor said strongly. "We cannot afford another round of sickness such as we have just experienced. I do not think we could survive it," she added bluntly.

"If you are up to it," Kell now said patiently, "we'll tell you something of our trip and what we discovered about the terrain." Kell picked up a stick and began to make tracings in the sand. "Look here." He drew a line. "This is about where the *Moonraker* went into the cavern, on the westerly side of the island."

········▶ MOONRAKER'S SURVIVORS
ROUTE TO SARAH'S BOSOM

── ── ▶ THE SEARCH TO
FIND MUSGRAVE'S CAMP

ENDERBY

ISLAND

Sarah's
Bosom

Camp

DISAPPOINTMENT ISLAND

Rock
formation
here
survivors
first
stop

AUCKLAND ISLAND

Moonraker
wrecked here
in sea cavern

Musgrave's
camp

They nodded, remembering well those grim, forbidding cliffs, rising sharply from the fierce sea. Kell's stick traced new lines in the sand.

"We headed northeast." He made a large X. "And we spent our first night here, on this rock. We then went on to Disappointment Island, which was about here." Again he placed an X to indicate the spot. "Then," his stick moved rapidly in the sand, "we rowed north, came into the bay, here, and made camp on Sarah's Bosom."

Willis was growing restless. "We know all that."

"I want to give everyone a picture of the layout of the land," Kell explained. "When we went searching for Musgrave's camp, we found a number of inlets along the easterly shore. When the weather and our health permitted, we did some exploring.

"For the most part, as we walked about, looking for Musgrave's hut, we found the surface to be very rough. Hills rise almost from the edge of the beaches and go on in a row of ridges and gullies. They're covered almost to their peaks with scrub. I've no doubt there are deep ravines behind the cliffs on the west coast, but we didn't get that far, of course."

"That first day, after you left," Chance interrupted. "I tried to remember the charts we had on the _Moonraker_. Captain Laws had shown me maps of the great circle route, showing the Snares and the Aucklands. He mentioned, just in passing," Chance ran his fingers hard across his brows, as if to force the captain's words to the forefront, "that the Aucklands were volcanic islands, about twenty-four miles or more from north to south, and in some few places, only about three miles wide. I remember, too," Chance went on gloomily, "that the captain said the islands were not fit for human habitation."

There was silence.

Not fit for human habitation.

The words weighed down upon Cat as if they were made of stone. He stirred restlessly.

"Well then," Kell said, fiercely, "we shall have to prove the captain wrong. It's true each day brings a new battle. We live from hand to mouth. The weather is our enemy. But we've seen enough of the land now to know that there are small forests of hardwood and pine — wood for building, wood for burning. There are grasses and ferns and scrub of every description. And thank God we do not lack for fresh water. That is plentiful."

"There is more," Bessie Taylor added triumphantly. "Wait." She left them abruptly, running back to the hut.

"What's she up to?" Billy wondered. "The way she talked, you'd think she had good news of some kind. What's she up to, Cat?" Billy repeated.

Cat furrowed his brows, trying to remember. Bessie Taylor had tried to tell them her news . . . something she had found. She had been excited, but they hadn't cared about anything, turning their faces to the wall to shut out the world. She should have been angry with them, Cat thought now, his face burning at the memory of how he had shouted at her to let him be. They had been poor patients. Illness had made them indifferent, and her words had spun out of their minds. If she was upset, she hadn't complained. She had just sighed and continued to tend to them.

"Can't you answer a simple question?" Billy asked shortly as Cat remained silent. "Never mind," he added, "she's coming back."

Bessie had emerged from the hut, holding something aloft that glinted in the sunlight.

"Here," she said breathlessly, thrusting a bottle into Kell's hands. "When I was out hunting, I came across a tree with a name carved on it. The *Victoria*. And under it there was this bottle with this paper in it."

Kell pulled the paper from its glass container.

"What is it? What does it say?" Gullitt asked eagerly. "Does it tell us how to get back to New Zealand? Is it a map?"

"No. It only states that goats and rabbits have been left on the island. Along with some pigs."

"Oh!" Billy was bitterly disappointed. 'Is that all?"

"Is that all?" Bessie Taylor said sharply. "Is that *all*? Don't any of you realize what this means? Somewhere on this island there is wild game. We will have something to eat other than seal and birds."

"Pigs! Pork!" O'Shea's face was wreathed in smiles.

"Rabbits," Kell mused. "We can surely use their pelts for warmth."

There was a lifting of spirits.

"Well." Willis said it for them all. "It seems as if Mr. Kell is right. We may certainly prove that Captain Laws was wrong about the Aucklands not being fit for habitation."

"What about Musgrave's camp?" Cat broke in impatiently. Wasn't that what they wanted to know?

"I take it, Cat," Spencer Gray commented, "that they didn't find it."

"Then you take it wrong." O'Shea grinned. "We were saving the best for the last. Find it we did."

"The hut itself is not what we expected," Kell took up the story. "But we found the walls lined with canvas . . ."

"Canvas! We can make clothes," Bessie cried.

"Or sails for a boat," Slush said with hope.

"We found an iron pot," Billy said gleefully, "and *nails!*"

"An ax, a spade, a file, and two knives," Kell rounded off the list, and waited for the reaction of the others.

Knives! They would not need to depend upon stones for cutting, or for scraping the skins of the seals.

"Worth their weight in gold they are," O'Shea said happily.

Cat looked up and caught Slush's eyes fixed upon him. Each knew the other was thinking of a dead man's gold, buried in the ground thirty feet from the sea that had nearly claimed it along with the *Moonraker.*

9

The Tattooed Ghost

Spencer Gray was busily braiding long blades of the tough grass. At his side, Cat was braiding grass as well, but his fingers did not move as nimbly.

"You work twice as fast as I do," Cat complained.

"Why not?" Gray answered reasonably. "I have been doing it twice as long as you." He looked over at the net Cat was fashioning from the grass. "I do not think either one of us can make a net like the one the Maori god Maui made to trap the sun."

"Why did he want to?" Cat asked with interest.

"To slow the sun as it crossed the sky, so men could have longer days. I am not like Maui. I don't want to slow the sun. I will be very happy if we can just snare the goats!"

It was Cat who had discovered them, who had come shouting into the campsite after a hunting expedition, so excited his words had tumbled over one another.

"Deer tracks. I saw deer tracks!"

"Deer? On the Auckland Islands?" Omar Chance had shaken his head slowly, half-closing his eyes as he did so. "Not possible, Cat."

"I did! I saw them. Come on. I'll show you the tracks."

"There can't be deer on the Aucklands." Chance was sharp.

"Well," O'Shea said reasonably, "the lad's seen something. I say we find out what it is."

Kell, who had been making needles from the bones of the albatrosses, put his work aside. "Show us the tracks, Cat. Lead on, and O'Shea and I will follow."

Now, in the middle of August, three months since the castaways had come to the island, some paths had become well worn from their feet as they went about the daily routine of hunting and fetching water. But now Cat left the usual path and was following a trail that had obviously been made by animals.

"Look," Cat pointed triumphantly. "Deer tracks. Lots of them."

Kell dropped to his knees, and O'Shea crouched beside him.

"Seeing that I've never stalked a deer in my life," Kell commented, standing up again, "I'm not the one to say what manner of tracks these are."

"Goats' tracks, if you ask me. You'll remember Bessie — Mrs. Taylor — finding the paper in the bottle that said there were goats on the island?" O'Shea asked.

"Bessie, is it, MacCool? Is that the way your mind is turning then?"

"I'll not hear a word against her," O'Shea cried, bristling with ready anger.

Cat regarded him with amazement. "But Mr. O'Shea, nobody's said anything against Mrs. Taylor at all. Why would they?"

"I've heard Gullitt talking. Aye, and young Billy, too. Talk not fit for your ears, Cat. Nor for mine," he added ominously. "And if you don't put a stop to it, Johnnie, than it's myself that will do it and the sooner the better."

They were following the trail south and west as they talked.

"Save your breath for the climbing," Kell said. Away from the beach, the land was hilly, rising sharply to fairly high peaks, and then dropping away almost as sharply. Between the hills, there were small valleys, more like gullies that had been scooped out by the winds that swept over the island.

"How much farther do we have to go?" O'Shea asked

Cat, but Cat had come to a halt when they reached the summit of the second hill.

"There!" Cat pointed. A herd of animals was feeding quietly below.

"Bless the lad. He's found us food on the hoof."

"Not deer," Kell whispered, as if the animals could hear him. "Goats. Wild goats."

Kell and O'Shea searched the ground carefully for heavy sticks. Then, hefting them in their hands, they stole down the hillside as quietly as they could. At their approach, however, stealthy as it was, the goats scattered in terror, some racing swiftly up the side of the next hill, others milling about in confusion, bleating loudly.

"Sure, I'd have to be a goat myself to catch one of the creatures," O'Shea gasped after a while, winded, his breath so shallow and rapid his chest ached.

Kell did not answer. He had his eye on a young kid, bewildered and frightened, crying as it fell behind the others in the flock. With an extra burst of speed, Kell caught up with it and felled it with a blow from his club. Cat turned away, repelled, but Kell forced him to turn his head back and look at the young animal lying still on the ground.

"You'll not go squeamish on me now, young Cat," he said, his face grim. "That's food you're looking at. Food!"

"Aye, food," O'Shea repeated, coming up behind them. "And how do you think meat came to be on your table at home in Boston, eh, laddie? Did not someone kill an animal to put it there?"

Kell lifted the animal to his back. "It's a grand find

you've made for us. A change in diet."

"It's sick I am, I can tell you," O'Shea added heartily, "of blubber and roots and gooney birds. And seals, too!"

"It may be our only diet for a while if we can't find seals," Kell reminded them grimly. Seals had been in short supply in the month and a half since Kell and the others had come back from their search for Musgrave's camp. He added, to comfort Cat, "We'll not be killing all that we catch, I hope. Goats are the poor man's cows. We'll be wanting to keep some for milk, and if we can figure out how, maybe we'll even make cheese."

"Cheese!" Cat's eyes glowed.

"I make no promises," Kell added hastily.

When they returned to the campsite, they were greeted with cheers. Skinned and roasted over the open fire, the young kid provided the castaways with a fine meal.

"There must be a better way to catch goats," O'Shea groaned. "I tell you flat out, if I'm to chase goats as we did today, we'll not be dining this way often."

It was then that Spencer Gray suggested that nets be woven from the grass and volunteered to show the others how to make them.

"Could the nets be used to catch fish?" Bessie Taylor asked.

"A remarkably fine idea," O'Shea said quickly, and fell silent at once when Bessie Taylor smiled at him warmly.

So it was that Spencer Gray and Cat were making nets. Bessie Taylor took over the task of cutting long thin strips of sealhide to be used as thread, as soon as they were able to discover how to make the sealskins pliable enough to be used for clothing.

The makeshift clothes they had cut, using the canvas from Musgrave's hut, were beginning to wear thin and become ragged.

How did one make a hide soft? They had tried everything. Gullitt had suggested rubbing the skins with sand. Willis had insisted upon scraping them with stones. Omar Chance had worked doggedly with a knife. They had soaked the skins in salt water and then in fresh water. The hide that served the seal so well resisted every attempt they made.

And then Kell had suddenly come up with the answer. He scraped the fur as closely to the hide as he could without cutting into the skin. Then he rubbed the hide with melted blubber, working the animal fat thoroughly into the skin. He then hung the skins on drying racks, stretching them until they became soft and pliable.

"That's the way the American Indians cured hides," Cat remembered. "Ned told me that once."

"Oh, Cat," Bessie Taylor said, reproaching him. "Why ever didn't you say so before this?"

"Because I never thought of it until after I saw what Mr. Kell did." He felt guilty and then thought, why should I feel bad? I can't remember everything Ned told me about the Indians! I didn't always pay that much attention!

"We know how now, and that's what's important," Chance said. "Now we can all soften hides."

"I'll be the tailor and cut the pieces," Kell said, grinning, "but we'll all sew."

Some sewed during the day while others hunted or stockpiled bracken for the fire or brought water to the camp. Some sewed by the light of the fire in the evening. The work went on, as swiftly as possible, for the thought of warm clothing was like an unexpected gift.

Cat was used to thinking of August as summer — hot and sticky — but August in the Aucklands was forbidding; winter still held the island in an iron grip.

"So much has been done since Mr. Kell came back," Cat told Gray. He was thinking of the new shelter that had been built, larger and more comfortable than the other hut. Seven of the castaways now lived in it. The old hut was used by O'Shea and Kell, with one portion of the hut screened off with branches to give Bessie Taylor privacy.

There had been some argument.

"Why you two?" Gullitt had demanded.

"Call it the royal guard," O'Shea had replied, staring at Gullitt until the other dropped his eyes and walked away.

"You like Mr. Kell, don't you, Cat? And respect him, too."

"Yes, sir, Mr. Gray. I do. He's like a captain on a ship. He always seems to know what to do. And he knows how to make people do what they're supposed to do. Even Mr. Gullitt. Do you think there will be trouble between Mr. O'Shea and Mr. Gullitt?" he asked suddenly.

Gray's fingers grew still. "What kind of trouble?" he asked, keeping his voice matter-of-fact.

"I think Mr. O'Shea is in love with Mrs. Taylor.

And I think she likes him, too. And I think Mr. Gullitt
. . ." His voice trailed off. "I don't like the things he
says about her." Cat kept his head down. His face
flushed.

"I imagine you've heard this kind of talk before,"
Gray said, very quietly. "You can't live on board ship
and not hear a lot of things you might not choose to
hear, Cat."

"I know how men talk. It's . . ." Cat's shoulders
hunched. "You get so you don't pay attention to it.
But this is different. It's Mrs. Taylor . . ." He looked
down at the grass he was still automatically braiding.
"I wish there was some way we could get off this island." Because if we don't, he worried, there will be
trouble.

Spencer Gray went back to the weaving.

"Our only hope is a ship, and how do we get a ship to
come here if no one knows we're on the island?"

"Then we ought to let them know somehow," Cat
cried.

"And how do we do that?"

"I don't know," Cat answered miserably. "I've finished my net." He held it up for inspection. When
Spencer Gray approved it, Cat picked up one of the seal
bladders. "I guess I'll go fill this with water." He
wanted an excuse to go off by himself, to sit on a large
rock overlooking the sea, his "thinking" stone for the
times when he was troubled, or unhappy, or needed to
be alone.

"It's a good idea," Gray said gently.

He's an understanding man, Cat thought as he picked
up the seal bladder and moved off. Different in the

way he understood things from Mr. Kell. Mr. Gray might never be able to take charge, the way John Kell did. But he had a feeling for other people's needs. Like now, Cat felt, knowing that he had to go off, even if it was for only a little while. And Spencer Gray would continue to weave his nets, and there would be no blame or disapproval in his glance when Cat returned.

Cat made his way directly down toward the beach, veering off before he reached it; a group of rocks formed a small wall that ran to the sea. Cat walked along the wall until he reached the last boulder. It had a fairly smooth surface. Cat imagined that perhaps it was a favorite spot for some seal, or had been until humans had come along. Now it was Cat's.

He sat down and watched the sea. It was quiet enough at the moment, but it would not last. Far off the wind was probably whipping rollers into a frenzy, making the water froth.

I don't want to think about anything, Cat told himself, just look at the water. Absently, he played with the bladder, rolling it in his hands. Then, without realizing what he was doing, he put the bladder to his mouth and began to blow into it. Slowly, as air flowed into the bladder, it began to expand. It looks like a ball, he mused as the bladder stretched wider. He held the end tight, to keep the air from escaping. Looking down, he saw a long fiber of grass caught on his pants. He pulled it free and tied it securely around the enlarged bladder.

Just then a gust of wind tore it from his hands. He

reached for it but missed. The wind carried it aloft and out to sea. Cat strained to see it as it moved farther and farther away. When it was gone from view, he shrugged. No one will see it again. Maybe some sailor might, though, and wonder what it was and how it got there.

Cat froze. Then he let out a whoop of joy and went tearing back to the camp.

"I've got it," he shouted. "I've got it. A way to get a message out." He was so excited he was stammering.

Everyone crowded around him, catching fire from his excitement.

"Catch your breath, laddie," O'Shea said and immediately urged, "Speak up now. What way have you in mind?"

"Mr. Kell," Cat said. "You know how you say everything can be put to some use?" He didn't wait for an answer. "Suppose we scratched out a message on a piece of wood — a small piece — and tied it to a bladder." He saw the look on their faces. "I mean, first we blow it up, then we tie it, and tie on the message. The wind will carry it . . . it *works!*" he shouted. "I just did it, and the wind carried it way out to sea. A ship could see it. It could. I know it could . . ."

They didn't believe him. It was in their eyes. They didn't even want to try.

But then Kell spoke up. "It might work. And we've nothing to lose by making the attempt. You've a good head on your shoulders, laddie. Let's find us a smooth flat piece of wood."

"You're serious." Gullitt couldn't believe it. "You're

going to play games with . . ." He was angry. "And we're going to drop everything to try out . . ." Again he couldn't finish his sentence.

"I'll try anything that will get us off this place," Willis said, his voice rising. "I'll find you a piece of wood, Mr. Kell."

"How will we put the message on the wood?" Bessie asked, in a practical manner. "And what will we say?"

"As to that, we can scratch it on the wood with a nail," O'Shea suggested.

"The message could be short," Omar Chance added. "Something like . . . Help! Survivors, the *Moonraker*, on Aucklands."

Willis had returned, smoothing the surface of a flat piece of wood. The others watched as Kell laboriously scratched the suggested message on its surface. Then Spencer Gray selected a bladder and inflated it, tied it, as Cat had done, with a grass fiber. Again the others watched intently as Kell secured the message to the bladder.

"Now for the launching," Billy said eagerly.

They all trooped after Kell who held on to the bladder tightly to keep it from being tugged free by the wind. He did not want it blown inland. Only Gullitt remained behind, since it was his turn to guard the fire. He would not have accompanied them in any case, he told them, on such a fool's errand.

They might have been a group of picnickers, standing on the beach, unleashing a balloon that the wind picked up and sent soaring upward.

"It works, Cat. It really works," Billy shouted. "Look at the way the wind is sending it sailing."

They looked at one another and laughed. The bladder was swirling in space, almost a gay note in the gray sky, the wooden message bobbing in the air.

"How far do you think it will go?" Willis asked, watching the improvised balloon dip and twist and turn with each gust of wind.

"If we're lucky, until some ship spies it out," O'Shea said, expressing everyone's hope.

"Look," Bessie called. "Even the birds have come to watch."

Two petrels, skimming through the air, examined the strange wingless creature dancing in the sky. They wheeled about, uttering hoarse cries, challenging the newcomer in their domain. Then, suddenly, the petrels attacked the balloon, spearing it angrily with their beaks. On shore, the group fell silent as the punctured bladder fell and was carried off by the sea.

One by one they moved slowly back to the campsite. Cat's face was set, his lips pressed together in bitter disappointment. Bessie Taylor started to speak to him but thought better of it. Spencer Gray walked at Cat's side. He, too, kept his peace. There were times when even the kindest of words left wounds.

Gullitt was nowhere to be seen.

"He's gone and left the fire untended," Slush snapped, glad to have someone to vent his anger upon. "The fire could have burned out." He added more bracken to the flame, keeping up a steady undercurrent of mumbling.

The others went back to what they were doing before the adventure of the inflated bladder. There was almost no conversation; each person seemed to stay slightly apart, building a fence about himself with his own thoughts.

The clothing was finished — pants and jackets for the men and for Cat, a long skirt and jacket for Bessie Taylor. Bessie had helped Kell make hats. She went into the hut to don her new clothing; the men hastily changed where they were. When she came out of the hut, a smile trembled on her lips.

"I think," she said, running her hand down along the sleeve of her jacket, grateful for the warmth of the fur, "that we may start a new style in fashions."

Cat didn't feel like smiling, but he, too, like Bessie, couldn't help laughing. They looked so odd.

"We look like crumpled bags with feet," he said.

"Are there clothes for me?" Gullitt demanded, coming back to the campsite.

"Where the devil have you been?" Omar Chance barked at him. "And who gave you leave to take off and abandon your watch?"

"Nothing's happened to the fire. While you were playing with your new toy, I did some scouting on my own. Saw something the other day, and decided to go back and take a closer look."

Kell and the others weren't the only ones who could make discoveries, his manner seemed to say.

"And?" Chance demanded.

"Two miles due east northeast, Mr. Chance. A hut. And something you'll have to see for yourself."

Though it was not his watch, Slush elected to stand guard over the fire. Willis growled that he had had enough excitement for one day, and Bessie Taylor decided to stay behind as well. The others, however, followed Gullitt's lead. He refused to answer questions, just telling them to wait and see what his discovery was.

It had begun to snow, very lightly, large flakes that faintly dusted the underbrush and scrub a powdery gray white.

Finally Gullitt halted and pointed. "There's the hut."

They stopped and stared. There was nothing unusual about the shelter. It was what they saw standing in front of the hut that amazed them.

"It's a totem pole," Cat said, walking closer to examine the tall sculptured post guarding the hut.

"No." Spencer Gray contradicted him. "It is not your American Indian totem pole. It is Maori. See the scroll work?" He pointed to the base of the pole. "And the spiral designs? This carving you see in the buildings of my people. The lizard there in the center. That is Whiro, symbol of evil and death. And there at the top," they followed his pointing finger, "the face of the man with the tongue hanging out. Maori."

"How did it get here?" O'Shea wondered. "Was it brought here from one of the Maori villages in New Zealand then?"

"No," Gray said decidedly. "This post was carved here, on the island."

"With what?" Billy Smithy asked. "With a knife? Maybe whoever made it left a knife in the hut."

"No knife. Most likely with a *pounamu*, a piece of greenstone jade. It is often used as a tool blade by the Maoris because of its hardness, and because such a stone can be given an edge sharp as a razor."

"Strangest thing I ever saw in my life," Gullitt said bluntly.

While the discussion went on, Cat slipped around toward the back of the hut. He thought he had noticed something moving, swinging slowly as the wind tugged it.

Yes! He had not been mistaken. The hind part of a seal swung from a tree branch, turning slowly. Cat approached the tree cautiously and reaching up, put his hand on the seal meat. It was fresh. Someone had cut it not too long ago.

Another castaway, Cat thought. But why has he never tried to find us? He must have seen the smoke from our fire, heard our voices. Wouldn't someone living alone be desperate for the company of other human beings?

Hearing a sound behind him, Cat whipped around, and felt his heart turn over in his body. A figure stood a short distance away, tall and gaunt, the white hair long and wild, the face so heavily tattooed no bit of skin remained untouched. Cuts and grooves swirled from cheekbones to chin, decorated the broad nose, and bit deep into the forehead. Soot remaining from the burned gum of a kauri pine had been pressed into the tattoos. From the large ears, elongated greenstone jade earrings dangled. A black and white feather was thrust in the old man's hair, just above his left ear.

As the old man stared at him, Cat, on a sudden impulse, pulled his greenstone jade from beneath his jacket and held it so that the old man could see it. The old man, imitating Cat's gesture, pulled his own *pounamu* — a larger, brighter piece of jade — from around his neck.

He held it outstretched in the palm of his hand so that Cat could study it.

Not a word was spoken. The old man had appeared, like an apparition, seemingly out of nowhere. Now, as Cat regarded him in frightened silence, the other lifted his hand in farewell and appeared to melt into the brush behind him.

So Slush had been right after all, Cat thought. Slush had seen a ghost, and now Cat had seen him, too.

10

Will You, O Son, Survive?

An argument that had started at the hut grew louder and more heated when the castaways were back at their own campsite again. It had begun because Spencer Gray had forbidden the others to enter the hut.

"I've already been inside," Gullitt had shouted in anger. "Don't you tell me what I can do."

Gray had turned to Kell. "I am Maori. I know from the designs on the post and the designs carved above the doorway that this hut shelters a Maori chief." He pointed to Cat, who had come running back to tell them of the man he had seen. "And from Cat's description, the man is a *rangatira* — one of the leaders among my people. The home of a chief is sacred." When Gullitt began to protest, Spencer Gray said fiercely, "Would you allow anyone to enter your home at will? Does the home of a chief deserve less respect?"

Kell's decision had been made on the spot.

"We will not trespass."

"Agreed," Chance said immediately.

They had returned to the campsite, but when they were there, Gullitt had taken up the quarrel again.

"It's a better hut than ours. And I saw a number of things inside we could use. He's only one man — an old man, from what Cat said. What could he do to stop us from taking over?"

Gray said, with contempt, "My people were valiant warriors before the continent of America was discovered. We fought English soldiers in the early 1840s, and we fought them again just a few years ago. They learned our strength in battle . . ."

"We're talking about one old man," Gullitt interrupted, "so we don't need a history lesson."

"You went there alone," Gray answered. "If he had wished it, he could have killed you, that one old man. If he wished it, he could kill us all off, one by one. Would death be less final because it came from the hands of one old man?"

Gullitt was silent.

"Would the chief understand any English?" Cat asked with hope. He would be someone new to talk to, someone with interesting tales to tell.

"My people have been trading with English and American whalers since the late 1700s," Gray replied drily. "They have had time to learn."

"But what is he doing here?" Bessie Taylor asked with interest.

Before Gray could answer, Slush demanded, "Maoris are sailing people. Would the chief know the way back to New Zealand?"

"It's likely. Certainly, my people know the Snares well. They hunt there often, in April and May, for the young muttonbirds. They have come to the Aucklands, too, from time to time. In fact," he added thoughtfully, "one group of Maoris tried to build a settlement here, about twenty-five years ago, I believe. They didn't stay." He glanced around. "You can understand why."

"Would he be willing to be our navigator?" O'Shea asked.

Gray shrugged. "How can I speak for the chief? It is a long way back to New Zealand . . ."

"Only about three hundred miles."

Cat's eyes widened with surprise. Billy Smithy had said it so casually. Only three hundred miles. And just a quarterboat to cover those miles in, Cat told himself.

But now Slush took up the cause. "We could do it," he insisted eagerly, "if we knew in which direction to go."

"We could work on one of the quarterboats." Chance was thinking out loud. "Make it seaworthy. Rig sails for it from sealskins. With sails and a wind to billow them, oars to guide the boat and to row it when the wind slackened, and a navigator on board to guide us, we could do it."

Cat, listening, felt hope surge through him. Here, beside the leaping fire, warmly dressed in their fur clothing, it began to seem like a reasonable idea. He

111

could see the others responding to the idea, too.

Only Kell seemed resistant, warning, "It's too risky. Three hundred miles of open sea?"

"Musgrave did it," Gullitt argued.

"He was an extraordinary seaman . . ."

"How do you know the old man isn't an extraordinary seaman too?" Slush pointed out. "Is there any reason to think he isn't?"

"Is there any reason to think he is?" Bessie Taylor asked quietly.

"It's a lot we're taking for granted," O'Shea commented. "And all we're doing, that I can see, is running around in circles like a puppy chasing its own tail. We have a Maori among us. Who better to speak to the chief and ask him straight out, will he or won't he?" He turned to Spencer Gray. "Would you be willing to speak for us?"

"He may not return to his hut for some time, now that we have discovered it," Gray warned. "Finding him may take some doing. But when we can, Cat and I can seek him out. The Maoris love young people. The chief may talk to Cat, may even agree, if Cat asks him."

Later, Slush sought out Cat. Checking to see that no one was close by, anxious not to be overheard, Slush whispered, "Cat. I want to have a word with you. Meet me where the three stones line up. You know the place I mean." He winked.

"Where you buried . . ."

Slush covered Cat's lips quickly with his hand.

"Think it! Don't say it!" he blazed.

Wondering why Slush wanted this meeting, Cat slipped away as soon as he could do so unseen by the others. He was joined in a short while by Slush, who got right down to what he wanted of Cat.

"I mean to be one of the men who sails in the quarterboat," he said straight out.

"One of the men?" Cat repeated. "But wouldn't we all go?"

"Not likely. Not with Kell so strong against it. One of the quarterboats will go. And with Kell's sense of fairness," he said bitterly, "he may pick the men by lot. And what chance would I stand then? No, when the times comes, I'll be on that boat."

"But you don't even know if the chief would be willing to be the navigator," Cat pointed out reasonably.

"Which is why I wanted to talk to you," Slush replied. "You ask a man to do you a favor, and he thinks, why should I? What's in it for me? That's human nature, Cat," Slush warmed to his theme. "Nothing for nothing. But!" Slush caught Cat's arm, pulled him closer, lowered his voice, the expression in his eyes secretive. "Offer a man gold! Eh, Cat? Offer him gold, and what does he say then?"

"Gold?"

Slush jerked his head toward where he had buried the dead man's treasure.

"Say you promised the chief some nuggets. It would be worth it, Cat." He licked his lips. "And when we got back, we could get another ship and look for the *Moonraker*. We know where she went down. She could be salvaged, Cat. All that gold. And a fortune in precious stones as well. We could be rich, Cat."

Slush was beginning to make Cat feel uneasy.

"You said, back on the ship, that all that gold would be the curse of the *Moonraker*."

Slush was almost dancing in his frenzy to convince Cat.

"That was then," he said reproachfully. "I've had time to think since we've been here. And I'm not the only one. Gullitt dreams of it. So does Billy." He lowered his voice. "And Mr. Chance is in with us, too."

"Mr. *Chance?*" Cat found it hard to believe. Gullitt, and Billy, and Slush. Yes. They seemed likely conspirators to Cat. But the mate? Cat shook his head.

"Aye, the mate, too," Slush insisted. "Many times we've talked about going after the gold when we get back. Only up to now, that's all it's been. Talk. But now we can make it happen."

"I promised to ask the chief anyway, if we can find him . . ."

"Put it to him about the gold right off, Cat. Start with the best argument in the world. You do that for me, and there will be some gold in it for you too."

Cat shrugged. He started to tell Slush that gold was worthless on the island, no better than the rocks, and not nearly so precious as the water or the food or the fire, but he knew it wasn't worth the effort. Slush seemed obsessed. Instead, Cat turned away, to face the sea.

There was movement on the horizon! He stood rigid, hardly believing what he saw. Then he yelled, "Slush! A ship! A ship!"

Slush followed Cat's pointing finger. There it was, a

vessel actually moving steadily, some distance away, but seemingly headed for the island.

"Run and fetch the others," Slush ordered. "I'll stay here and keep my eye on it."

As if, Cat said to himself, the ship would disappear unless Slush stood on the beach and willed it to come closer.

His news brought everyone at the camp on the run.

"Quick!" Kell said imperatively. "Into the boat! We've got to get her attention!"

Willis, Gullitt, O'Shea, Chance, and Kell were first to scramble for the boat and reach it. They strained at the oars, sending the boat fairly skimming across the rough water.

On shore, the castaways watched as the boat seemed to be closing the gap between itself and the ship.

They could see Willis waving his arms about wildly, could hear the shouts of the others as they tried to attract the attention of someone — anyone — on board the ship. But the ship sailed on serenely. In a short while, it disappeared as silently as it had come.

The men brought the boat back to shore, their faces sullen with sick disappointment.

"The devil take you," MacCool O'Shea screamed suddenly after the vessel. "May you break your back before ever you reach a shore again!" Tears of frustration filled his eyes. He brushed them away roughly. "You've done us no favor, Cat Rider," he said, turning on Cat. "Better never to have seen her at all than to have hope so cruelly raised."

"You're not to talk to him like that, MacCool O'Shea," Bessie Taylor flared. "If they had but once looked our way, we could have been picked up, and it would have been thanks to Cat if we had."

"It only proves my point," Gullitt insisted. "Why should we sit by and wait for some passing ship, which may never come, when we have the means at hand to help ourselves?"

"We need that old man," Slush agreed, sending Cat a meaningful glance. "He has to agree."

"We'll start doing some work on one of the boats to-morrow," Chance said. "It will take a lot of work before it's ready."

"It's the wrong time of year," Kell told them. "If a boat is made ready, it could not leave until the summer, not until sometime in December, I would say."

They looked at one another in dismay. *December!* That was still some three and a half months away.

"But we can be thinking about it," Willis said. "And I think Gray and Cat's duties should be shared among us so they can be free to track down the Maori chief."

The others agreed.

So it was that Cat and Gray spent day after day in their search, always checking first to see if he had come back to his hut.

"He could be anywhere," Cat said, with frustration, when two weeks had gone by in fruitless hunting. "He could be watching us right now and laughing at us. He must know this island better than we do."

"We won't find him unless he wants to be found." Gray sounded weary.

They were standing on the peak of one of the hills, turning their heads slowly, trying to spot any move-ment anywhere, in any direction. Nothing moved.

Suddenly, on impulse, Spencer Gray threw his head back and shouted in Maori:

> *Bestir yourself*
> *So that you may reach the sacred mountain waters*
> *of your ancestors;*
> *A mantle 'twill be for you*
> *in the warriors' ranks.*

Cat didn't understand what Gray was saying, but the words sounded proud and challenging.

Both waited and listened, but there was no response. Slowly they turned, ready to walk down the hill. And then, as from a distance, they heard an answering cry:

> *Will you, O son, survive*
> *these times of bitter strife?*

And there, on another ridge, Cat and Gray saw the old chief, standing like a figure carved from the rock on which he stood, his hand raised in greeting.

11

Journey into the Shadows

You!" The old man pointed his finger accusingly at Cat. "You are *pakeha!* Why do you wear the sacred stone?"

"*Pakeha?*" Cat turned to Spencer Gray.

"The Maori word for white man," Gray explained.

When they had first approached the chief, he had spoken only in the Maori tongue, pretending that he knew no English, but before long he dropped his game, wearying of talking with Cat though a second person.

Now his eyes bored into Cat's, black and piercing beneath his wrinkled lids, the markings on his face seeming to deepen and intensify. Curiously, Cat was not afraid even though the markings were even more terrifying to behold this close.

"The stone was a gift, from Mr. Gray," Cat replied.

Chief E Kehu glared at the younger man.

"He is of the people," he said, still addressing Cat. "What is his true name?"

"Tell him my mother named me Epikiwati."

The chief nodded, impatiently. "Epikiwati gave away the sacred stone? He does not believe in its powers?"

"Oh no," Cat cried, shocked. "Mr. Gray has faith in the stone. He wished to save my life." Cat looked directly into the old man's face, meeting his stern gaze without flinching. "I believe in it, too, even though I'm *pakeha*, as you say."

It was true, Cat told himself. Seamen held many beliefs. No one who sailed the sea, who lived in that special universe of water and sky, was untouched by its legends and tales and superstitions.

"Why does the *pakeha* come to me?"

Cat's mouth felt dry. So much depended upon the chief's answer to their proposal. At the camp, the others had watched Cat and Gray leave, knowing that they were meeting the old man at last. They had con-

118

vinced themselves that their only hope lay in persuading the chief to act as their navigator. All of them had spoken to Cat, laying the burden of their hopes on this mission.

"We're survivors from the *Moonraker*," Cat began. "We've been here since early in May. Some of the men want to take the quarterboat and sail back to New Zealand and get help. They want to know . . . they told me to ask . . ." Cat bit his lips, then said in a rush, 'Would you be our navigator?"

"No!" E Kehu sounded angry. "I am *tapu*. I cannot go back." When Cat appeared puzzled, he added, "*Tapu!* Forbidden!"

He rose to his feet, making a gesture of dismissal, and entered his hut.

"Isn't he going to explain?" Cat asked Gray, taken by surprise by E Kehu's abrupt leaving. "Isn't he going to talk to us anymore?"

"Another time perhaps. Not now."

"Why is he *tapu?*"

Gray shrugged his shoulders. They had begun to walk back to the campsite, Cat dragging his heels, knowing how disturbing his news would be to the others. "A man may be *tapu* for many reasons. He will talk to you more freely if I am not there. I think you should visit him alone."

"Suppose he won't talk to me?" Cat asked with a worried frown.

"He will talk to you. It is the nature of our older people. It is how the Maori legends are preserved, by word of mouth, from grandfather to father to son."

Slush was first to see Gray and Cat returning. He

waylaid Cat as Gray kept on walking to the camp.

"What did he say? Why? Why did he say no? *Tapu?* Forbidden? Didn't you offer him gold, the way I told you to?"

"You don't understand." Cat began to feel exasperated by the way Slush was pounding away at him with his questions.

"I understand you were asked to do one little thing, that's all. One little thing. And you couldn't even do that."

Some of the others felt much as Slush did.

"What do you mean, he doesn't want to leave the island?" Gullitt demanded. He sounded offended, as if the chief's decision was a personal insult.

"Leave the boy alone," Bessie Taylor interfered. "He's done his best. You can't force someone to do something against his will. For whatever reason, the old man wants to stay on the island. I expect we'll have to accept his decision."

"Why?" Billy was pacing in agitation. "Why can't we force him to show us the way? It's not right, one man holding out against so many others for some silly idea he has in his head. Aren't our lives worth something? He's condemning us to the island."

"I think we are all getting too excited," Kell observed.

Cat could see that Kell did not like this new feeling that was sweeping over the men, this restless, hostile emotion directed at an old man.

"Chief E Kehu likes Cat," Spencer Gray told the others. "Why don't we wait and see what happens? Cat can visit the chief often. Maybe he can persuade him to change his mind some other time."

"Would you be willing to do that, Cat?" Omar Chance asked gravely.

Cat nodded. "I'll go back as often as he'll see me. And I'll keep asking."

"Now I have another suggestion to make," Chance said. "I'd like to take some of my men and move on to Musgrave's camp."

"Some of *your* men?" Kell repeated.

Slush, catching Cat's glance, winked. Didn't I tell you? Slush's smile seemed to say. Cat felt betrayed as if Chance had been guilty of disloyalty.

"He's still our first mate," Gullitt put in quickly. "Billy and Slush and me . . . we want to go and stay at the old Musgrave camp for a while, and the skipper has agreed to come along."

"Why?" Kell asked Chance.

"They've convinced me that the sealing is better there. They feel, too, they would be more likely to attract the attention of any passing ship there."

"And the real reason?" Kell's eyes were searching, going from one face to another, almost as if he suspected what Cat already knew, Cat thought.

"If you want to know," Slush burst out. "To get away from doing this little chore and that little chore because you think it's what we should be doing."

"Will you not need to be eating at the other camp?" O'Shea demanded. "Is the life to be easier somehow where you're going?"

"We plan to work on the quarterboat, to make her ready for the trip." Chance spoke as if some final decision had been made. "If we stay here, our time is too much taken up with other things. Down there, we'll work on the boat and on as little else as possible."

"And you can't stop our going," Gullitt said defiantly.

"When will you leave for the other camp?" Willis wanted to know.

"Any day now. We're coming into spring," Chance replied. "The weather's warming up. The sun, when it's out, stays longer. Winter's over, almost."

Cat realized that it was true. Though spring was nothing like spring as he remembered it back home in Boston, there was a different, a lighter feeling in the air. The rain, when it fell, was still cold and penetrating. The wind was harsh. But the trees were beginning to bud with new life; the grass had a greener, more alive brightness.

Chance had one last statement to make. "Anyone who wants to join us is welcome. Willis?"

"Not me." Willis was positive. "I'm used to this place. I'll stick with Mr. Kell."

"I'm staying." Spencer Gray agreed with Willis.

"Until you leave," Kell announced, "we do our assigned tasks as before."

It was Willis's week to tend the fire and do the cooking. The men scattered; Bessie Taylor went down to the beach to get sea water. The salt supply was running low. Chance and the others would need to take salt with them. She was concentrating on her task and did not hear Gullitt until he was very close.

"What do you want?" she asked sharply.

"You," he answered directly. "I want you to come to Musgrave's camp with us. I want you to be my woman."

"Stand aside, Mr. Gullitt. I have work to do."

"You haven't answered me," he insisted.

"I find you offensive, and your suggestion revolting. Is that sufficient answer?"

"I've been thinking about you for a long time, Bessie, and I'm a man who likes to put his thoughts into action."

Bessie's eyes swept the beach.

"We're alone," he said. "I made sure of that."

"Cat is just beyond that rock, looking for birds' eggs. He'll have heard everything you've said."

"Cat." Gullitt laughed. "You expect that boy to come running to interfere with me?"

Cat was behind the rock and had heard everything that had been said. He had stiffened when Gullitt had spoken so bluntly to Mrs. Taylor, and his face was flushed now with anger at Gullitt and embarrassment for Bessie. He bent down and picked up a large stone. Holding it in his hand, he came up over the rock, ready to hurl his makeshift weapon at Gullitt. But he found his help was not needed. Bessie Taylor had swooped down, grabbed a stout stick, and had laid Gullitt flat on the beach with a well-aimed blow to the side of his head.

"I expect," she said to Cat as he came running to her side, "that Mr. Gullitt's head must be ringing."

Gullitt sat up, bracing himself against the sand on one elbow.

"You *hit* me!" His surprise was mixed with sullen rage.

"I'm no dainty little lily in the field," Bessie Taylor warned. "I ran a boarding house for miners after my husband's death. They are as rough a bunch as you fancy yourself to be, Mr. Gullitt. And some with the same fine approach as yours," she added with scorn.

He picked himself up and left without another word.

"I'll run tell Mr. Kell and Mr. O'Shea," Cat said, looking after Gullitt.

Bessie put out her hand. "No need, Cat. You'll only upset them. Mr. Gullitt will not be bothering me again. I've damaged his pride. Besides," she added practically, "he and the others will be leaving soon, and the problem will be gone with them."

Cat felt that he ought to tell Mr. Kell, if not O'Shea, but since Mrs. Taylor was so positive, he reluctantly agreed to keep the matter between just the two of them.

Two days later, Chance, Gullitt, Smithy, and Slush got into the quarterboat and left for Musgrave's camp.

"Talk to the chief," Slush called to Cat. "And remember what I told you."

Cat nodded.

"Be sure you guard the fire," Kell warned. Chance had transferred some burning bracken to the old iron pot they had found on the first trip to Musgrave's hut.

"He's like an old mother hen." Billy kept his voice low, and then fell silent when Chance sent him a forbidding glance.

"When will you be back?" O'Shea asked.

"As soon as the boat is seaworthy. Probably toward the summer, say the end of November," Chance promised. He studied the quarterboat, which had been generously supplied by the other castaways. "And when we come back, we'll hope to hear good news from Cat about the chief."

Every eye swiveled in Cat's direction.

"I'll try," Cat promised. "I'll really try."

"Fair enough," Chance agreed.

The remaining castaways watched as the boat pulled away. There was a feeling of sadness in the air. It was as though the first step had been taken on a journey hidden in shadows.

12

Find the "Pohutukawa" Tree

CAT ENJOYED THE TRIPS they had begun to make to Enderby Island. This was a small island that lay close by, north of the main island. Enderby Island, unlike the main island with its sharply peaking hills and narrow gullies, lay low, intersected with belts of scrub except where there were sand hills. It was on these sand hills that they first caught sight of rabbits, and Kell, busy planning for the winter although it was still spring, spoke of building rabbit hutches.

The south side of the island bristled with nettles. On this side of the island, they had found the McQuarie cabbage and some few potatoes, which they had used as seed to grow new crops.

Here, too, in the all-too-short spring, they had enjoyed the quiet beauty of daisies and buttercups interspersed in patches of white clover.

The northwest side of Enderby was steep, and though lichen and moss dotted the peaks of the scattered hills, no grass grew there. The island, they discovered, was no more than about a mile and a half at its widest point, nor more than three and a half miles in length.

On the main island, when summer came, in late November and December, their hearts had been gladdened when the belts of rata, or ironwood, which fringed the shore burst into bright scarlet blossoms. Miles of blooms gave them a sense of the seasons, no matter how brief the time of flowering.

Cat visited Chief E Kehu often. Though the old man rarely smiled, Cat knew the chief was happy to see him. At times they sat without speaking, and Cat would watch E Kehu's knife carving intricate and beautiful designs into wood. Other times E Kehu spoke of times past, of the history of his people, of the seven canoes of the Maori ancestors that had come a great distance across the water to find the land of the long white cloud — *Aotearoa*, the land that the *pakeha* called New Zealand.

When Cat touched upon personal matters, the chief grew cold and angered. But Cat persisted.

"Are you my friend, Chief E Kehu?" Cat asked one day.

"I am friend to the one who wears the greenstone jade," came the grave reply.

"Can a friend not know why the chief is *tapu?*"

"Once I was a warrior, a great warrior. The English came to our land, from their far-off country, and they wished to take away our land. Then the Maori put on their battle dress of feathers and paint. I followed King Tawhiao, I and the other warriors of our *pa*." The *pa*, Spencer Gray had once explained to Cat, was the fortified village in which Maoris lived.

"We followed King Tawhiao and lined ourselves up before the fort. White settlers were hiding there." E Kehu pointed to the fierce face on the post before his hut. "Do you see how the tongue hangs out? So E Kehu and the other warriors stuck their tongues out at the settlers and the soldiers, making faces, rolling our eyes, to frighten them. And we chanted our war songs."

E Kehu's eyes glittered, remembering.

"The English soldiers had not enough food. So our king stopped the fighting and sent his best men to the *pa*, to bring food and drink to the enemy."

"You did that for your *enemies?*" Cat was amazed. "Is that why you are *tapu?*"

"No, no." The old man's memories saddened him, Cat could see. "That was long ago, before your eyes opened upon this world. No, two years ago, the people fought the English soldiers again. E Kehu," he placed a trembling finger upon his chest, "was old, but his heart was still that of the warrior. And then E Kehu was taken in battle." His head dropped. "I was freed, but my shame remained. To be taken prisoner — that is *tapu*. So I came here, so my people would not be shamed by my presence in the *pa*."

"But things are different now . . ."

"Some things do not change."

"You could be a guide and then come back. You could save all our lives," Cat said persuasively.

"You have the sacred stone. You will be safe," E Kehu said.

"But . . ."

The old man held his hand up, palm facing Cat, his eyes grave.

"When I leave this place, it will be to make a special journey. Far to the north on *Aotearoa*, there is a high ridge of rock which hangs over the water. On this ridge there is a tree — the *pohutukawa*. It holds fast to a crevice in the rock. It is there, down the roots of that tree, that the spirits of those who have died glide into the sea, into the underworld of *po*. Some say the spirits rise again as birds to fly home, to the ancient land of our ancestors, to Hawaiki. Some say the spirits are swept to the horizon on the last glimmering rays of the setting sun into eternity. E Kehu will make this journey soon. The spirit of E Kehu will fly home."

Cat's eyes grew wide. The meaning of what E Kehu was telling him suddenly became clear.

"You're not going to die!" Cat cried.

"Why does E Kehu's friend grieve when E Kehu does not?" the old man said gently.

"I have to go back now." Cat's voice was unsteady.

"Do not speak of this to your companions," E Kehu requested. "The stories E Kehu speaks are not for the ears of others."

Cat walked back to the campsite, his mind in a daze. What would he tell the others — Gullitt and Chance and Slush and Billy — when they came back? What he had told them when they left, he supposed, only that the chief still refused to go with them.

When he arrived at the camp, it was almost as if his thoughts about them had brought them back, for he found that the four men had finally returned from Musgrave's camp. Chance was describing to Kell and the other castaways what they had done to the quarterboat.

"It's a good sound boat." The quarterboat was twenty-two feet long by four feet six inches beam. They had taken down the sealskin sails they had used at first. They had found canvas in another abandoned hut. Using the canvas lining, they had fashioned a jibsail and mainsail, Chance explained. It had taken them a long time. The work went slowly, for their fingers were frequently numb from the cold, even in what passed for summer on that island.

They had picked apart the rope that held the beams of the hut together, oakum it was, a kind of loose hemp, and had remade it into smaller, tighter ropes.

"Tedious work," Chance went on, "and it took all the time left of the day after each day's hunt for food."

"We made a forward bulkhead." Billy took up the story. "Constructed it out of timber from the hut, and covered it all over with sealskins, to make it waterproof."

"She's a tidy craft," Willis agreed, who had inspected the boat carefully when the men had returned.

"You'll need lots of supplies." Bessie Taylor was thinking out loud. "Water, of course. And as much food as you can comfortably store."

"Who's to go and who's to stay then?" O'Shea wondered. "Will we be drawing lots?"

"No!" Gullitt was emphatic. "We fixed her up. It was our idea. It will be the mate, Billy, Slush, and me."

"Better to draw lots," O'Shea repeated. "Fairer. What if the boat is lost at sea?"

"No lots. We'll take that chance," Slush said, drawing his lips together into an obstinate line.

Chance changed the subject. "I noticed you have a pen with some goats. I counted nine kids in the pen. You've been busy since we left."

"We've blankets, moccasins, extra clothing . . . thanks to Mr. Kell and the seals." Bessie laughed.

"And Mr. Gray found the root of the McQuarie cabbage, over on Enderby Island," Cat put in. "Mrs. Taylor made a paste from it, a kind of flour."

"And in the evening, we play cards," Willis said in an offhand manner, watching carefully to see what the reaction would be.

Gullitt stared. "You do what?"

Willis grinned. "We play cards. We found an old bread locker on one of our foraging trips. And since Mr. Kell will allow nothing to go to waste, why I took the tin lining and cut it into fifty-two pieces, and scratched the emblems of the cards on them with a nail. Took me two weeks. Mr. Kell kindly excused me from my duties for that time so I could make them."

"*Kindly* excused you from your duties?" Gullitt repeated in a sarcastic tone.

"Aye, kindly," Willis snapped back.

"Look." Cat spread the cards out for the others to see. "We've been playing cards every night. And Mr. Willis made dominoes for us, too."

Willis nodded. "I put together a fine set of shells. You can see how I've marked them. It's another good game to play in the evenings."

"Very cozy," Slush said. "For those who plan to stay on the island. But that's not for us, is it, Mr. Chance?"

"When will you leave?" Kell asked.

"I think sometime within the next three weeks, while it is still December and summer. For that's what we'll need, a good sunny summer day."

"Then the sooner we get the supplies laid on, the better," Kell agreed.

"What about the chief?" Slush asked. "Have you talked to him?"

"Again and again, Slush. But it's no use. He won't go," Cat said.

Slush pounded the fist of his right hand into the open palm of his left with frustration.

"He's got to come. We can't sail without him."

"Then why not give up the whole idea?" O'Shea wondered. "You've no compass, no charts, no clear idea in which direction to sail."

"Musgrave did it." This was Gullitt, who could not seem to understand that there was not a man among them who was likely to repeat what Musgrave had accomplished.

"We're back to that again," O'Shea sighed.

"You take me to that chief," Gullitt said confidently. "I'll soon change his mind for him."

"No. I won't." Cat was openly defiant. He knew Gullitt's methods of persuasion.

"All right." Gullitt lifted his hands in the air. "But

you could ask him to come down when we're ready to ship out. You could do that, couldn't you, Cat?"

"What for?" Cat was still suspicious.

"Because it might be lucky for us," Slush said, "even if he's just standing and watching. Maybe he wouldn't mind pointing us in the right direction. Now that's not too much to ask of anybody."

Cat examined the idea. Something — some feeling he could not explain — made him uneasy. But he could not put his finger on what caused the feeling. At last, reluctantly, he agreed to persuade the chief to come and watch when the boat was ready to leave.

There now began a bustle of preparation. Everyone pitched in willingly. Bessie Taylor, with Slush's assistance, baked a whole seal and one of the goats from the pen. Willis, using the gulletts of seals as water containers, stored better than thirty gallons of the precious liquid on the boat. Cat and Billy hunted for the eggs of seabirds, collecting thirty dozen. These were boiled and, together with some salted seal, were put aboard wrapped in sealskins.

At last the boat and the men were ready, but now the weather held out. Day dragged after slow day. It was the middle of January in the new year of 1867 when a bright clear summer day dawned, quiet and calm, with just the hint of a breeze.

"This is the day," Chance announced.

"Go and get the chief," Slush yelled at Cat. Cat nodded and ran off. To his surprise, when he had first mentioned it, Chief E Kehu had agreed immediately to come to the beach to watch the four *pakeha* sail away.

The castaways gathered solemnly on the beach.

There was a heaviness of spirit weighing on their hearts. They had had their difficult times, and there had been clashes between them. But they had shared a common fate, a common struggle to stay alive.

"Here they come!" Billy shouted, first to see Cat approaching with the Maori chief. The old man walked erect and proud beside his young companion.

"Chief, come see our boat," Gullitt called good-naturedly. "See what we've done to her, how we've fitted her up for the passage back to New Zealand."

The chief hesitated briefly, then, stepping away from Cat, moved closer to Gullitt. When he was within reach, Gullitt seized him and placed a knife against the old man's throat. "Better still, chief," Gullitt muttered, "get on the boat."

"No!" Chance called out, his eyes blazing with anger. "That was not part of our plan. Release the man at once."

"You're the mate," Gullitt said, "but I respectfully beg to tell you that the chief goes with us. Insurance, Mr. Chance. If you don't like it, you can stay here with the others. But the old man comes with us, either way. Am I right, Billy? Slush?"

The answer was in their faces.

Without turning, Chief E Kehu told Gullitt, "I wish to give something to the boy, to give to Epikiwati."

"He means me," Gray explained.

"Let the boy come forward," the chief insisted. As Cat approached, the chief removed the greenstone jade from around his neck and dropped it into Cat's hand.

"Have no sadness," he told Cat. "The time I spoke of is at hand. I go to seek the *pohutukawa* tree."

Billy and Slush clambered into the boat. Chance walked by Gullitt without a word and took his own place aboard. Gullitt, the knife still at the chief's throat, backed them to the boat, where they stepped in, helped by the others.

Those on shore watched the boat leave in grim silence. Soon a fresh breeze sprang up. Before long, the boat was a faint dot on the horizon.

Cat's hand closed over the greenstone jade the chief had placed in his hand. He felt a sense of overwhelming loss. He did not notice that the others had left the beach, or that Spencer Gray had moved close to his side.

"Did you understand," Gray asked at last, his face saddened, "what E Kehu meant when he told you of the *pohutukawa* tree?"

Cat nodded.

"Some say the spirits rise again as birds to fly home . . . E Kehu will make this journey soon . . ." Cat could hear the old man's voice in his memory.

Cat hoped the Maori chief would find the *pohutukawa* tree, that his soul would sweep to the horizon on the last glimmering rays of the setting sun . . .

"Into eternity," the old man's voice sounded again in Cat's mind.

Into eternity.

Wordlessly, Cat dropped the greenstone jade into Spencer Gray's hand and walked away.

13

"God Give You Wings"

"I HAD A DREAM last night," MacCool O'Shea announced one morning, as the castaways gathered round the fire for breakfast. "It was my mother, rest her soul, come to me in my sleep."

"And what meaning do we take from that?" Kell asked, encouraging O'Shea to continue.

It was the beginning of March; six weeks had gone by since Omar Chance and the others had taken to the sea in the quarterboat, six weeks of waiting, impatient, anxious waiting, with the castaways on the island abandoning their tasks to rush and gaze off eagerly to sea, discussing endlessly all the possibilities: the quarterboat had reached the Snares and had been found by Maoris; no, the men had been picked up by some ship at sea; nonsense, they had done what Musgrave had done, sailed directly to Stewart Island, that most southern portion of New Zealand, and even now a rescue ship was on its way to the Aucklands.

A vicious storm had arisen that same night after Chance and Gullitt and the others had left. The quarterboat must surely have gone down, taking all hands with her. But next morning, the sun had been brilliant; the day had been extraordinarily calm. Good seamen with a superb navigator along — what was a bit of nasty weather to them? They were safe . . .

The conversation among the castaways was on a permanent seesaw; hope soaring upward, hope plummeting swiftly downward like a bird shot out of the sky.

O'Shea continued: "She looked me in the eye and she said, 'Paddy love, you'll be leaving this island, for a ship will be coming by . . .' She was that real," O'Shea's voice was filled with wonder, "I could almost reach out and touch her. 'Paddy,' says she, in that soft loving way she had, 'take heart. 'Twill be a brig that comes to fetch you away from this place, and she'll have Maoris on board her.' And with that she faded away."

"Maoris?" Willis laughed, a short barking sound. "What would an Irishwoman who never left home know of Maoris?"

"What difference does it make?" O'Shea roared. "Do you not get the sense of what I've told you. We're to be saved. 'Tis an omen!"

"An omen." Willis glowered. "Omens and good-luck stones. They could have been there and back, except they've been lost at sea, drowned all of them, the mate, Gullitt, Slush, Billy, the old man. Not a living soul anywhere in this world knows we're here, and you talk of omens, and the boy and the Maori cling to their jade stones." Willis rose, casting his food aside. "The only way we'll get off this island is by dying." He left them abruptly, his shoulders hunched, his head lowered, to wander down to sit on the beach and stare blankly out at the sea, a solitary brooding figure.

Behind him he left a pall of gloom.

It was then that Kell came to a quick decision. Before the others left, Kell made his announcement.

"I think it's time for us to leave the main island and move to Enderby," he said briskly.

"Move? Why?" Cat asked, echoing how the others felt. What difference did it make where they stayed on the Aucklands?

"The hunting is better there. We've got a good potato patch going on Enderby now. The rabbits are in good supply. We'll build a new shelter."

"You just want to keep us busy," Cat accused.

"Would you rather sit about and feel sorry for yourself, like yon Willis?" Kell replied, in a cutting voice.

"When will we go?" Bessie Taylor asked.

"Now."

"*Now?*" Her surprise was mirrored on the faces of the others.

"Summer, such as we had of it, is gone," Kell explained patiently. "The weather is already beginning to bluster. The sooner the better."

They ferried their supplies to Enderby, tending the fire carefully, knocking down the two huts to bring the timber to their new quarters.

Willis and Gray were sent on a foraging expedition. In the ten months the castaways had been on the Aucklands, they had continued to find items that Kell had pressed into some use. Cat had asked Kell how it was that they continued to turn up odd bits and pieces, and Kell's explanation had been reasonable. The Aucklands, Kell had told Cat, had, long ago, been tried out as an experimental whaling and sealing station. Huts had been built that had long since fallen apart, abandoned far back in the early 1800s when the Aucklands had proved unsatisfactory as a permanent station. Many things had been left behind, useless to the sealers and whalers.

"We know about Musgrave's wreck," Kell had continued, earnestly. "But how many other ships have lost their lives here, eh, Cat? Could not other survivors, like ourselves, have lived here? We've no way of knowing, have we?"

"Do you think Mr. Willis and Mr. Gray will find something we can put to use on Enderby?"

"Why not, lad? You can search a place a hundred times and find nothing. And then you can go back and stumble into good fortune. You have my word on it. Such things do happen." Kell sounded positive, but even he was stunned when Willis, his black mood gone, came smiling back to camp, accompanied by a happy Spencer Gray.

"*Bricks?*" Kell breathed, not quite believing it. "And *tiles?*"

"I fell over them." Willis grinned at their expressions. "Caught my toe and fell right smack down on the ground. I thought it was a root sticking out, or a rock."

"And when I went to help him, I dug around the spot," Gray began, but it was Willis's find and his story.

"You should have seen us. Tore the ground away with our bare hands. It was like finding gold!"

Cat's thoughts flashed to Slush, and the dead man's gold he had buried, then dug up, and taken along with him when he left the island. Where was the gold now? Had the sea claimed it after all?

"But where did the bricks and tiles come from?" Bessie demanded. "It's like a gift from heaven!"

"A gift from the Maoris." Gray's smile deepened. "We just happened to stumble . . . at least Willis did

138

. . . over the old Maori settlement. What do you say to a genuine chimney in the new shelter, Mrs. Taylor. A Maori gift to the *pakeha!*"

The new shelter, a house twenty feet by eleven, with one corner set aside and screened for Bessie Taylor, did indeed have a genuine chimney. When the shelter was finished and the fire was burning properly in the chimney, they congratulated one another formally and then broke into gales of laughter.

The date of the moving was carefully scratched into a new "calendar" stone. March 15, 1867.

It was a sobering date, a reminder that this would be their second winter on the island.

"Only now," Cat said, speaking their thoughts aloud, "we're much better prepared for winter, aren't we?"

"We'll be warmer; we have shelter; we have food."

"We have knives, thanks to Johnnie." Kell had cleverly made knives from the shovel they had found. Using a file, he had cut the shovel into six pieces. These were to serve as knife blades. Heating one end of each, he had driven a nail through, making a hole for the handle. He then had tempered them by plunging them into red-hot oil. O'Shea had sharpened the blades against a hard rock, honing them to a fine edge.

"And we have our woodpile always ready," Bessie Taylor reminded him.

Kell nodded. Spencer Gray had carefully constructed a *mai-mai* on the highest hill on Enderby. An enormous stockpile of wood had been stacked near it. Each day one of the castaways, including Bessie Taylor, went up to the *mai-mai* and stood watch. Ships did not normally pass this way, but it was a possibility not to be overlooked. Smoke on the island would surely be spotted from the sea.

Their appearance had changed greatly, but they had grown so used to one another, they scarcely noticed the changes. The beards of the men were long and ragged, although they hacked away at the growth from time to time with their knives. Their hair was wild, falling below their shoulders. Cat, whose fourteenth birthday had come and gone unmarked, was taller. He was lean, but appeared heavier because the hard work had built his muscles powerfully. He had lost the young boy look he had had on the *Moonraker*.

It was in the middle of April that they spied a sow feeding close to the water as they were rowing along the beach, close to the main island.

"A sow!" O'Shea cried, puzzled. "Where did she come from?"

"The *Victoria!*" Cat remembered it well, the day Bessie Taylor had told him that John Kell and the others had come back from their search for Musgrave's camp. It was when they had all fallen so ill, and Mrs. Taylor had cared for them. He remembered how she had run into the hut and come running out again, holding a bottle high in her hands. Kell had pulled the paper from the bottle; it had stated that goats, rabbits, and pigs had been left on the island. "You said 'Pigs! Pork!' don't you remember, Mr. O'Shea?"

"And I'll say it again," O'Shea shouted gleefully.

"Easy," Kell warned. "Keep your voice down, Mac-Cool. We don't want to scare her away."

He and O'Shea and Gray stalked the sow cautiously.

"Now!" Kell shouted. The sow squealed and attempted to flee, but the men brought her down. They came back to Enderby Island in triumph, and were greeted like returning heroes from battle.

"We'll dig pits. There must be other wild pigs about." Kell was full of plans as the sow was roasting over the fire that night. "We'll take the boat out again tomorrow and dig a series of pits."

"I'll come with you," Willis offered. It was his turn to stand the lonely watch on the summit but Kell did not make an issue of it. Better for Willis to be with them and kept busy than to be muttering to himself in the lonely shelter on the hilltop.

"I'll take the watch," Cat offered.

"Well," Bessie Taylor said practically, "while you go out and dig pits, I'll continue to sew clothing for us. I wonder how seals use their hides for a lifetime but we wear them out in a few short months."

"If seals lived the way we do," Cat said, "they'd have a mother seal off somewhere making new hides for them."

Bessie laughed. What a picture that was!

That night there was easy talk and laughter around the fire burning cheerily in the fireplace. Only the smallest change in the routine, Cat thought, studying his companions, and our hopes spring up again.

The pits were a failure. The pigs fell into them, but climbed out again before the men could catch them.

"Nothing goes right," Willis muttered. "We might just as well forget about the pigs."

Forget about the pigs? Not John Kell, Cat decided, seeing Kell lost in study, his eyes with that unseeing gaze that spoke of the mind busy behind them.

"If we can't catch them in pits, we'll go fishing for

them," Kell announced, after a long period of silence.

"Fish? For pigs?" Spencer Gray's eyes danced. "Your mind has finally snapped, friend."

"Fish for pigs?" O'Shea echoed. "Now then, Johnnie, what's this about?"

"I'll show you all tomorrow," Kell replied mysteriously and would not say another word.

The next day, their duties laid aside while they waited to see what Kell's plan was, they watched as he heated some old pieces of iron they had found in one of the abandoned huts. He then began to shape them into hooks. Willis and Gray helped, once they realized what Kell was trying to do. When the hooks were ready, Kell boiled them in oil made from seal blubber to temper them.

There was much good-natured comment that Kell accepted amiably, continuing to work steadily according to the plan he had thought out the night before.

"Maoris are such good weavers," Kell said presently to Gray. "Can you weave me a goodly length of fiber grass? Mind now, it has to be strong."

While Gray wove the fibrous grass, Kell had a new request. "Find me some poles." Willis, his interest caught in spite of himself, brought Kell a pole some twelve feet long. Carefully, Kell took the hooks and attached them loosely to the pole. He then took the grass rope Spencer Gray had made, which was about eighteen feet long, and just as carefully tied the grass rope to eyeholes in the hooks. At last he stood up, stretching to ease his cramped muscles.

"Now then," he inquired casually, "is there anyone for going fishing?"

"I'd not miss this for a month of Sundays in Ireland," O'Shea vowed. "It's a sight I'll be telling to my grand-children, the good Lord willing."

They all trooped after him. There was a feeling of being on holiday. For the moment, their situation was forgotten. It was a game, for all except Kell, who was in deadly earnest, and they laughed and joked as they followed him.

"Whisht!" O'Shea said, first to spy a large black sow with a litter of young beside her. "Look there, Johnnie. Now let's see you fish."

Kell clutched his fishing pole tightly. Slowly, care-fully, noiselessly, Kell crept up behind the unwary sow. Suddenly, with a quick movement, he thrust the hook into the sow's back, threw the pole down, and hauled away mightily on the rope. "I've got her!" he bellowed lustily. "I've got her! Quick! After the little ones."

The sow set up a steady stream of shrieks and wails; the young pigs squealed and fled in every direction. One, blinded with fear, ran directly into Cat's hands. He held the quivering animal, running his hand along the small creature's back, making soothing sounds.

"Help me with the sow, or she'll break loose," Kell called. Willing hands came to his aid.

Back at the camp, Kell decided that the sow, more frightened than hurt, would not be killed, nor the piglet resting somewhat more relaxed in Cat's arms.

"We'll build a pen," Kell said, "and keep her safe."

"Aren't we to eat her then?" O'Shea asked in disap-pointment.

"Not this one, MacCool. I'm thinking it's time we started a pig farm, don't you see." He grinned at

O'Shea's expression. "It will be a long winter. It would be nice to step out to the pen and choose dinner without having to exhaust ourselves first. And while we're at it, it would be a good idea to make a hutch now and keep some rabbits as well. Since we're to stay the winter, this one might as well be easier than the last."

"You can't start a pig farm with just a sow," Bessie reminded Kell.

"We'll find ourselves a boar then."

"Just like that?" Willis asked.

"Just like that," Kell said easily.

"It's because he has faith," O'Shea told Willis.

"It's because he has an iron will," Willis insisted.

"Since we're not to kill her, then she should have a name," Bessie suggested. "We had a cow on our farm in Ireland called Nellie."

"A beautiful name." O'Shea accepted it grandly.

In another month, Nellie had a mate, a huge, mean-eyed boar with coarse thick hair, who was promptly named Roger. In spite of his appearance, Roger took eagerly to domestic life. Both animals soon became tame, answering to their names, and gave every evidence of enjoying human companionship. As one or the other of the castaways came to the pen, Nellie and Roger would come close to be stroked. Kell's dream of a pig farm could now be a reality. The piglet, who became Cat's special pet, tumbled after Cat wherever he went. The adults, listening to Cat call every once in a while, "Here, Harold. Here, boy. Over here," would smile at each other. A boy and a pet — it gave them all a good feeling.

One evening, as they gathered together near the fireplace, Willis and O'Shea playing cards intently, Cat and Gray playing dominoes, Bessie looked about at the peaceful scene and said gratefully, "How much better off we are now than when we first set foot on the island. Our hut is fairly weatherproof." Mud and the tough tussock grass had been used to thatch the roofs. It kept the hut reasonably dry and cozy. Sealskins and canvas lining the walls kept the savage winter wind out. "We have needles and thread and skins for clothing. Shoes and hats! Buttons of wood and bone. Mufflers of rabbit skins! And what a blessing, Mr. Willis, that you found those two additional bread tins."

"Aye," O'Shea agreed. "And who but Johnnie Kell would look at a bread tin and see it as a lamp?"

Kell looked up from his work — he seemed to be concentrating on shaping a piece of spar — shrugged his shoulders and went back to whittling the wood again.

Cat looked at the lamp. It was a rough-looking light but very welcome. Kell had used twisted bits of flax, which grew in plentiful supply on the island, for wicks, and seal blubber for oil.

They had other — what had Mrs. Taylor called them? — amenities as well. Amenities! Dishes of wood, made by Spencer Gray, who was so good at carving. Forks and spoons from albatross bones, made by Willis. Those, Cat learned, were amenities.

They had all learned from Kell that everything found on the island, no matter what it was, could be put to some sort of use sooner or later.

"I'll tell you one thing," Willis said suddenly. "I'd

give the world for a cup of coffee — even that slop that Slush used to make."

Cat thought of Captain Laws and his constant demand for coffee. How long ago it all seemed — the ship in the cavern, that first desperate search for land, the struggle just to stay alive.

"My pipe, that's what I'd like," Kell said, almost wistfully.

"Pumpkin pie and a glass of milk," Cat said. His mother's fresh-baked pumpkin pie just out of the oven, his mother's face flushed from the heat of the stove, Cat remembered, and the milk poured from the pitcher frothing up to the rim of the glass.

"You're mighty quiet, MacCool. Have you no secret desire then?" Kell teased.

"Aye," O'Shea said quietly. "I've my heart's desire — to stand one time again before I die in a green meadow in Ireland in the spring, with the smell of the grass in my nostrils, and a whisper of rain in the air."

A mood of nostalgic sadness gripped them all. They abandoned their games; Kell stopped whittling.

> *The man in the wilderness asked of me*
> *How many strawberries grew in the sea.*
> *I answered him as I thought good*
> *"As many as red herrings grow in the wood."*

Bessie said briskly.

The others stared at her in annoyance. Her silly verse had broken into their mood.

O'Shea cried, "Strawberries in the sea and red herrings in the wood. What's the meaning in what you're saying, can you tell me that, now?"

"There's as much meaning in that nursery rhyme as in everything else we've been saying, sitting here, all of us, mooning about what we'd like."

"Mrs. Taylor is right," Kell agreed. "We can't afford to look back or it will rob us of the will to face life as it is now, the hard reality of it. There are only two courses for us now — to survive each day and to plan for the future."

"Plan for the future!" Willis said bitterly. "What future?"

Kell went back to his whittling. "We have a future. I place my faith in God and our will." He held up the spar and examined it with a critical eye.

"Is it toys you're make now?" O'Shea teased, coming close to see what Kell was doing.

"It keeps my fingers limber." Kell seemed abstracted again. The castaways knew that look well by now.

"You're up to something, Johnnie. Tell us straight out, what is it you're plotting now?"

"No more than what has always been on my mind. Our rescue. Willis is right, you know, MacCool, when he says there's not a living soul anywhere knows we're here. And comfortable though we may be," Kell sent a small smile at Bessie Taylor, "I mean for someone to know that we're here and to come and get us."

"I'm a handy man with a knife," Gray said. "Do you want help?"

Kell held up the spar. "I've fashioned the hull. Now it will need an iron keel heavy enough to ballast it in all weather."

"I don't understand," Bessie interrupted. "What do you plan to do?"

"I plan to make a small boat, put a plea for help on it, and put it to sea. Correction," he added. "Several boats, for if some are lost, others may be found."

"I'll attach the keel to the spars," Willis offered. "And she'll need a mast to keep her upright." Willis was caught up in the activity in spite of himself.

"And she'll need sails," Cat said, excited. "I can cut sails from bits of sealskin."

Kell shook his head. "No, laddie. I think not. We've some zinc. We'll give our boats zinc sails, because, don't you see, we can scratch a message on zinc."

"We can work on the boats all day tomorrow," Willis said eagerly.

"No. We've our tasks." The necessities of life took first place over all other things. It was a daily, monotonous grind, but it had to be done. Each day consisted of a continual hunt for food and firewood. The men would pair off, each with a knife and club, searching for seal. Days might pass before the hunt was successful. Only Sunday was set aside for resting. O'Shea spent that day withdrawn and reserved, in hopeful prayer. The men talked quietly, either around the open campfire, or, like as not, wandered off to the beach or climbed to the top of the hill to sweep the horizon watchfully for the sight of a sail. For Cat, it was a day of storytelling. Spencer Gray had a seemingly endless well of Maori tales to spin.

They had argued over the message to be scratched into the zinc sail. Willis had suggested: *Moonraker wrecked on Auckland Isles 14 May, 1866; 6 survivors to date. Want relief.*

"The message is as long as the begats in the Holy Book," O'Shea growled. "Johnnie will be forever and a day in the writing of it."

"The shorter the message, the sooner we put the boat to sea," Spencer Gray agreed. "Let's keep it simple."

Finally, Kell, using a heated nail, laboriously stamped out the appeal: *Help! 6 survivors Moonraker on Auckland Isles.*

The launching of that first boat was ceremonious. All went down to the beach. Kell, O'Shea, Willis, and Gray got into the remaining quarterboat and rowed a short distance away. Then Kell took the tiny boat, with its urgent appeal and held it above the sea for a brief moment before putting it down gently in the water.

The tiny craft bobbed about and then, caught by the breeze, moved out to sea.

"God give you wings," O'Shea called after it.

The craft moved on. They stared after it until it vanished from view.

14

Aaron Drew— Last Survivor

N0, HAROLD! NO!" Cat shouted. He was out of breath, his face flushed, his eyes bright and clear. Kell had inflated the bladder of a seal and made a rough football from it. It was a game they played on Sundays now, a game in which the pig took delight, racing in among the legs of the players, sometimes tripping them up as they ran.

Cat enjoyed playing football. Even Reid Willis caught some of the excitement of the game and joined in from time to time.

When the game was over, and they had flung themselves down on the ground to recover from the rough-and-tumble activity and catch their breaths, Kell had a proposal to make.

"I've been thinking," he commented. "I thought we might row over to the main island and then explore, starting from our old campsite, due west, to the northwest cape."

"What's there?" Willis was not in favor of starting out upon some new venture. They had settled in on Enderby Island well enough, he now grumbled, and why couldn't they just take things as they were.

"Oh Mr. Willis," Cat argued. "We've never explored that part of the island. And we could find something new. Don't you remember the day you found the bricks and tiles from that old Maori settlement?"

"Someone has to remain behind, to guard the fire," Bessie reminded them.

"Well, it seems that Willis here," O'Shea began, but Willis interrupted.

"No, if there's exploring to be done, then I'll go along."

"It's my week to cook," Bessie said. "So of course I'll stay."

"And I'll go on watch at the *mai-mai*," O'Shea offered.

For a moment it seemed that Kell was about to protest O'Shea's decision, but he merely said instead, "Then the rest of us will be on our way."

As they got into the quarterboat, Harold came chasing into the water after them, squealing and trying to swim after them.

"Go back!" Cat shouted frantically. "Pigs can't swim. Go back, Harold!"

Still Harold persisted.

"Thinks he's a dog." Willis grinned. "I guess you'll have to jump in and save him, unless you want him to drown."

Cat was already over the side, even as Willis was speaking. He pulled Harold to the beach, scolding him all during the rescue. "Now you stay," Cat said firmly. Harold shook himself thoroughly, meanwhile setting up a series of sad grunts.

"Poor Harold," Cat said, smiling, as he rejoined the others in the quarterboat.

He turned away from the sight of the pig, settling down on the sand to await their return, and thought about Bessie Taylor and MacCool O'Shea. Cat had seen how Bessie's face flushed with pleasure when O'Shea decided to stay behind, had noticed how O'Shea's eyes warmed at Bessie Taylor's smile.

"They're in love, aren't they, Mr. Kell? Mr. O'Shea and Mrs. Taylor, I mean. They ought to get married."

"Married?" Willis repeated with surprise. "Who's to marry them?"

"Mr. Kell could."

Now it was John Kell who was surprised. "I've no power to join a man and woman in holy matrimony,

Cat. Whatever put such a notion in your head?"

"Aboard the *Moonraker*, Captain Laws was the law at sea. He could do anything. You've been like our captain since we've come to the Aucklands. I thought that would give you the right . . ."

Kell shook his head decisively. "No, laddie. 'Twould not be legal in the eyes of man. Nor in the eyes of God. O'Shea would not accept it, nor would Bessie Taylor. Best not to be turning your mind to matters that don't concern you," Kell added, "or any of us."

When they reached the main island, they drew the quarterboat well up on the beach to secure it. They went past their old campsite, the others scarcely looking at it, but Cat stopped to linger for a moment. So many things had happened at this place. But it was not a time for looking back; he hurried to join the others.

They found the walking rough going. The underbrush was thick; climbing the hills seemed to take a greater toll of their strength than before. Willis fell twice, once cutting his forearm just above his wrist on a sharp rock. It was a jagged tear that did not bleed much but began to throb painfully after a while.

Cat, seeing how Willis nursed his arm, holding it up against his body, dropped back to join him.

"Are you all right, Mr. Willis?" he asked anxiously.

"I'm fine," Willis answered roughly. "You think I've never had a little scratch before? Move on. You don't have to keep an eye on me."

When he thought Cat wasn't watching, he rubbed his cut. Some fine grains seemed to have been pushed under the skin. He lagged behind the others, trying to work the grains out with his fingernails.

It took them several hours, but at last they were coming close to the northwest cape of the island. They could hear the sea.

Catching up to Kell, who seemed tireless, Cat asked in a low voice, so he could not be overheard, "Mr. Kell. Why did we really come out on this scouting trip? That's what it is, isn't it? A scouting trip?"

Kell looked down at Cat, considering his answer. "I was thinking. It was something that came to mind. Once, when I was talking to Mr. Gullitt about the Musgrave wreck, he mentioned that another ship had been wrecked along about the same time. Musgrave and his men were camped south; the men from the other wreck were camped north. They were within twenty miles or so of each other, and neither camp knew of the other."

"That's hard to believe, Mr. Kell!"

"Aye. But it happened."

"What happened to the men in the north camp?"

"I don't know. I expect they were rescued. I think we should spread out here," Kell now told them. "I'll head as far west as I can go. Gray, you go north. Cat, you and Willis go south."

They separated. Cat was sorry he had been sent with Willis, for Willis moved aimlessly, without interest, without making any attempt to study the ground. He just stumbled along, unseeing and silent, occupied with his own thoughts.

And yet it was Willis who stopped abruptly, so abruptly that Cat, his head turned, ran into Willis.

"What is it? What's the matter?" Cat asked, and then he, too, saw what Willis was staring at. A hut, only one wall still standing, sagging steeply to one side, was in a small clearing directly ahead. In front of the hut was the skeleton of a man, the skeletal legs encased in the shreds of what had once been trousers.

Willis stood absolutely still, his eyes riveted on the skeleton. After a moment, Cat began to shout for the others, hoping his voice would carry and bring them to this spot. He called and kept calling until first Gray and then Kell came running.

"What is it? What have you found?" Gray gasped.

Cat pointed.

Kell had arrived by this time.

"Search the area," Kell ordered. "Maybe we'll find something to tell us what happened here."

At first their hunt was fruitless. And then Cat found a rotted board. Examining it carefully, he called the others to come and look.

Scratched into the board were letters so faint they could scarcely be read.

Invercauld, May, 1864, Aaron Drew, last survivor.

"Last survivor." Willis' face had gone chalk white. His eyes seemed wild. "Who knows how long he stayed alive, after the others were gone?" He turned, ready to go crashing off through the woods, to escape this horror.

Kell, reaching out, placed his hand gently on the other man's arm.

"Will you not stay, Mr. Willis, and help us give the poor man a decent burial?"

Willis did not reply, but he stayed. They had nothing to dig into the ground, to make a grave, so they made do by covering the skeleton with brush and bracken, mounding it over the bones in silence.

"O'Shea should have come," Spencer Gray said at last. "He is a man for saying prayers. We should say something."

"The Lord is my Shepherd; I shall not want." The words sprang into Cat's mind, and he said them aloud in a faltering voice. They were the words the minister had spoken when Cat's father had died.

Willis, Kell, and Gray bowed their heads. When Cat was finished, Kell picked up a handful of dirt and scattered it across the new mound.

"Rest in peace, Aaron Drew," Kell said softly, "and God give you grace, wherever you may be."

Gray placed the board across the grave.

Willis was ready to leave, but Kell insisted that they continue their search.

"See what we can find?" Willis was shocked. "Why that's like robbing the grave."

"No!" Kell was sharp. "The man was long dead. As were the others who survived the wreck of the *Invercauld*. But we are *alive*. And I mean to see to it that we stay alive. Do I make my meaning clear?"

At first Cat felt as Willis did, but he had learned much since they had been wrecked and found their way to the Aucklands. The first consideration of the castaways was survival. To survive meant to face life however harsh its demands.

When they returned to their quarterboat, they were carrying a precious hoard of items: a wide, sharp cutting tool made of iron with a long wooden handle that

Cat called an ax — but Kell identified as an adz — an iron pot, a bread box, and an assortment of pieces of metal.

They also carried back with them something not obvious to them — a sense of deep depression, a mood that spread quickly to Bessie Taylor and MacCool O'Shea when they greeted the others on their return.

"Poor, poor man," Bessie Taylor said.

"Better to say poor, poor us," Willis exclaimed, putting into words what they were all thinking. Would this happen to them? Cat wondered uneasily. Would they die, one by one? Would Cat, as the youngest one there, survive them all, to be left alone on the island?

He shuddered at the idea. And when he went to bed that night, he could not fall asleep. His thoughts turned again and again to the man who had died alone and in despair, the man who had spent his last days scratching out the words — *Aaron Drew, last survivor.*

How different this was from the story E Kehu had told him; the old Maori chief who went peacefully to search for the *pohutukawa* tree.

Cat's eyes closed and soon he was dreaming. A white bird surfaced from beneath the sea. It shook its wings, then soared upward and flew off, turning golden red in the blazing brilliance of the western horizon, where the setting sun clung to the dying day.

"E Kehu," Cat, still dreaming, called to the bird softly, but the bird did not turn back. It kept steadily to its flight, and its rendezvous with the horizon.

15

Fly, Spirit, Fly!

WILLIS WAS ASLEEP. He had been ill for the past three weeks since he and the others had found the skeleton and buried it. The cut on his forearm had become inflamed and then infected; he had become feverish. The others had been helpless as his fever climbed and stayed high. Mostly, Willis drifted between stupefied wakefulness and restless sleep. That evening, however, it seemed to the castaways that Willis was much better. He was able to take some food and hold it down. He even seemed interested in the boat that Kell and Gray were making. O'Shea was tapping out the appeal for help on the zinc sail.

"How many boats does this make?" Willis asked in a whisper.

"The fourth." Kell glanced over at Willis and smiled at him encouragingly. "And maybe the one that will bring us all help. You'll be back on a proper ship before you know it."

"Would you try and take a little soup now?" Bessie Taylor coaxed.

"That would be nice," Willis agreed. "My mother used to make a hearty soup. It stuck to a man's ribs, her soup did."

There was a feeling of contentment in the hut now. It was the first time in days that Willis had spoken sensibly, taking an interest in things around him.

"Oh dear," Bessie said, when she came back to Willis's side with the soup, "he's slipped off to sleep again."

O'Shea moved to Willis's side and very gently began to rouse the sleeping man. "Willis, me fine bucko," he whispered soothingly. "Open your eyes, Willis. Open your eyes."

Slowly, Willis's lids fluttered. He looked at O'Shea without recognition.

"She was beautiful," he whispered.

Willis in love? Cat could not imagine that Willis had ever been young and in love.

"Good. You're awake," Bessie said. "I have some lovely broth for you."

Cat made a face. The lovely broth was seal soup, and it was horrible.

But Willis was still babbling.

"Like a bird. She rode the seas like a sea gull. Beautiful. Like a dream, with the sun going down, putting a glow on her sails, and shadows, deep purple shadows on the under curves of the canvas. The riggings looked like they'd been spun of silk. What a barque she was." Willis sighed.

Suddenly he sat up and said clearly, "You're to bury me at sea." He held up a hand weakly to quieten the rush of protests from the others. "A man knows when his time has come." His voice was weak but firm. "Many a ship lies in Davy Jones's locker, and many a mate of mine is asleep in the deep. Maybe my spirit will find me one last ship down there, and the captain will put us to hauling on a halyard or tramping round the capstan . . ."

"His mind is wandering again," Bessie whispered,

noting that Willis's eyes had glazed and seemed to be looking deeply inward.

". . . and we'll sing our chanties. Is that you, Mr. Chance?" He peered intently at O'Shea. "Captain's orders to put our weight on the capstan bar? Aye, aye, sir. 'Strolling the highway one night on a spree, hey-ho, blow the man down.' You're not singing, Cuzzen," he said reproachfully, to some long-gone shipmate. "On with it now."

O'Shea said huskily, "Sorry, matey."

"*I met a flash packet, the wind blowing free, give us some time to blow the man down.* You always did have a fine voice for the chanties, Cuzzen," Willis said approvingly, as O'Shea sang with him. "I don't hear Gullitt and Hayman." He looked around, his glance taking in Kell and Gray. "All together now, lads."

Kell nodded. Now they took up the chant.

"*I fired my bow chaser; the signal she knew; hey-ho, blow the man down; she backed her main topsail and for me hove to; give us some time to blow the man down.*"

Willis slumped against O'Shea's arm, his eyes staring, a small smile on his lips. Gently, O'Shea put his hand to Willis's face and moved the lids down over the dead eyes.

"Pray God grant him his last wish," O'Shea said, weeping.

"Will you help me weave a shroud for him?" Gray asked Cat quietly. Cat nodded, his lips trembling as he fought back choking sobs. He and Gray had woven nets from the fibrous grass before; it was the first time the weaving was for so sad a purpose.

Next morning, Willis's body, wrapped in the grass-woven shroud, was carried down to the beach and placed aboard the quarterboat. There, wordlessly, all five got into the boat and rowed about a mile out to sea.

The water was flecked with hurrying whitecaps; a single petrel, wings outspread, kept watch in the lowering sky. At a signal from Kell, the men slipped Willis's weighted body overboard. O'Shea, head bowed, began the words familiar to them all: "Our Father which art in heaven, hallowed be thy name . . ."

When the prayer was finished, they made no attempt to leave, as if by lingering they remained in touch with the man who had returned to the sea. Then, softly, Spencer Gray began to chant:

> *He goes to the land*
> *Of stillness and shadows.*
> *He does not hear our chant.*
>
> *Go, good friend, to the shadowland;*
> *To Po, the darkness that awaits you.*
>
> *You do not hear our prayer.*
> *You do not hear the beat*
> *Of our paddles in the water.*
>
> *Yet you will rise —*
> *From darkness to Ao;*
> *Your spirit will soar*
> *To the light.*
>
> *Fly, spirit, fly!*
> *You are free!*

Overhead, the petrel gave a shrill cry and followed them, as if reluctant to leave, as they dipped their oars in the water and rowed solemnly back to the shore.

16

The Whip

JOHN KELL examined the miniature boat he held in his hand, the fifth such boat he had made since first he thought of sending out these calls for help. He had worked steadily on the rough piece of wood, some three feet in length, blocking it out and shaping it, then attaching a heavy piece of iron designed to trim the tiny craft by the stern, to keep her before the wind. A short stout mast with a tin sail completed the vessel. On the deck of the craft he had carved the words *Moonraker May 1866 wrecked on Aucklands 5 survivors Sept. 1867. Help!*

Cat ran his fingers over the carved words.

"May 1866 wrecked, September 1867, five survivors," he repeated, dully. "Why do you bother? They're only lost at sea."

"We don't know that," Kell began in a reasonable tone, but Cat flared, "Yes we do. If a ship the size of the *Moonraker* can be lost, who's to care about this . . . this toy?"

This feeling of despair had been Cat's constant companion since Willis had died. When they had come back to the camp, after burying Willis at sea, Cat had said, "I guess it will be one of us next."

"No, Cat." The protest had come from Bessie Taylor. "He was an old man. And he had an infection we couldn't treat . . ."

"Why give the boy false hope?" O'Shea had snapped. "We'll be picked off, one by one, and if we don't join Willis in the sea, then it's the fate of others who've died here before us we'll be sharing before long."

"I'll hear no such talk." Kell's temper had blazed at them all alike. "We've done well and we'll do better. MacCool," he had coaxed, "you'll not be forgetting the dream you told us about?"

"The dream? What dream is that, then?"

"Why it was your own blessed mother, come to you in a dream, telling you we'd be rescued, remember, MacCool? By a ship with Maoris aboard? Do you mind it now?"

" 'Twas only a dream, nothing more," O'Shea had replied, turning away.

As a result of Willis's death, the thought of their dying off one by one took root in their minds and held fast. What if something happened, and one by one they did die? Who would wish to be the lone survivor?

Little by little, the castaways began to give up all pretense of doing their chores. If they went out, Gray or O'Shea or Cat were likely to drift down to the beach and sit on the sand, indifferent to the winter's bone-biting cold, staring blankly at the sea. If they stayed indoors, they huddled near the fireplace, gazing blindly at the leaping flame.

If they spoke to one another at all, it was to flare up into small, meaningless quarrels.

Of the five castaways, only John Kell and Bessie Taylor fought the gloom which surrounded all of them thick as the fog that sometimes invaded the island for days.

They moved in a trance, uncertain ghosts in a shadowed world.

"Will you help me launch the boat, Cat?" Kell held the boat out, but Cat kept his hands stubbornly at his sides.

"You could have saved us," Cat accused him now. "You're always full of ideas. Why couldn't you find some way to save us?"

"What do you want of me?" Kell cried out in frustration. "Can I wave a magic wand, then, and produce a ship on the horizon? Do you think I never grow weary? Do you think I never grow heartsick and sore from the battle to stay alive? Do you think the idea never comes stealing into my mind — have done, John Kell. Have done!"

Cat was ashamed. "I'm sorry, Mr. Kell," he said. "It's just that nothing seems to matter anymore."

"Come with me, Cat," Kell commanded. Out of habit, Cat followed Kell, who led the way to where Spencer Gray and O'Shea lay sprawled on the beach.

"On your feet," Kell barked. O'Shea and Gray stared at him but did not move. "I said on your feet!" Kell reached down and pulled O'Shea erect, and then yanked Gray roughly to his feet as well.

"We are going out in the quarterboat and we are going to launch this vessel. And if I have to beat you to a pulp . . . and I mean you as well, laddie . . . you shall do as I say. Do you doubt that I can?" he challenged them. He stood away from them a pace, curling his fingers into fists. "What's it to be then? Do you come with me willingly, or do you come bloody and bowed?"

Cat shuffled after Gray and O'Shea, getting into the

quarterboat, his face filled with sullen dislike for Kell. When the quarterboat had moved far enough away from the beach so the water could sail the tiny boat outward bound, Kell slid the vessel into the sea and then nodded for the others to turn back.

"Well, we've launched the fifth of your vessels," Spencer Gray mumbled. "Does it make you any happier?"

"Sure, don't you see the rescue ship sailing straight for us?" O'Shea sneered. His nostrils quivered, always a sign of rising anger in O'Shea.

Kell said nothing until the boat was secure on the beach again. "MacCool, was it not your turn to stand watch on the hilltop this day?"

O'Shea slumped to the ground. He didn't bother to reply.

"Come along, Cat. You and I will stand watch." It was an order. His feet dragging, Cat, with Harold trotting happily behind him, followed Kell up to the hilltop, where Kell checked the pile of bracken and grass near the *mai-mai*. Cat made no attempt to help; he simply sat and stared at the sea.

"Never let the hope die in you, laddie," Kell said, trying to help Cat break free from his prison of hopelessness. "Hope is a better companion than fear and a better friend than despair. As long as there's a breath in your body, there's room for hope."

"I don't want to talk," Cat said abruptly. Kell's harping on hope only made Cat feel more irritable. He's only saying the things he thinks I want to hear, Cat thought rebelliously. He got up and left; the pig trotted after him docilely, wandering off to inspect suspected treasures beside the path, then racing to catch up with Cat.

The next morning, Kell again called on Cat for assistance, this time asking Bessie Taylor to come along.

"What's happened to us?" Bessie Taylor asked as she walked to the beach with Kell and Cat. "Mr. O'Shea complains of increasing weariness. He walks a short way, staggers, and lies where he falls. If it rains, he makes no attempt to move. Mr. Gray's wrists seem to be swelling. And Cat hardly moves at all."

Cat was listening, but the words seemed to be a jumble in his mind.

"I think we have scurvy," Kell replied.

"What's scurvy?" Cat asked, but paid no attention to the answer.

"It's the sameness of our diet. No vegetables. No fruit," Kell explained. "And much of it is despair. Everyone's given up hoping."

"Where are we going? What are we looking for?" Cat asked, vexed. He wanted to sink down to the ground now, and not get up.

Kell held him firmly by the arm. "We're going to that stretch of beach that slopes upward. Just a little way further," he added encouragingly.

"I'm cold. I want to go back to the fire," Cat complained.

"All in good time. Now you can warm up by helping me search for wood. I want some good long pieces."

"Wood?" Cat repeated, as if Kell were speaking in some strange tongue.

"Wood," Kell said firmly. "Because you and I, Cat, aye, and Mrs. Taylor, too, are going to build a spring-board."

"A *springboard?*" Bessie was puzzled. "Whatever for, Mr. Kell?"

"I can do nothing about the scurvy," he replied, "but I can do something about the despair that keeps you all idle. You, Cat, start bringing the wood. And mind now, they are to be good long pieces."

Under Kell's direction, the springboard slowly began to take shape. It was no more than a narrow wooden platform that was built on the elevated section of the beach. From the end of the springboard, there was a three-foot drop. When the springboard was finished, Kell tested it. He ran along the platform and, when he came to the end, lightly leaped the three feet to the ground. Now he was ready for the second step in his plan.

"Cat. You have learned how to weave the grass with the skill of a Maori. I should like you to weave some-thing for me now."

"Another net?" Cat asked wearily.

"A whip."

"A whip?" The word made no sense to Cat. "A whip, like . . ." He made a flicking gesture.

"Surely you've seen a man with a whip in his hand when driving a team of horses?" Kell said patiently.

Cat thought Kell had gone mad. First he built a springboard that went nowhere, and now he wanted a whip. No, two whips! For, side by side with Cat, Kell sat and braided the longest, sturdiest grass fibers he could find.

At last the whips were finished. Kell tested them in the air, making the grass whip hum as he snapped it experimentally.

And then Kell made his announcement. "I have built a springboard down at the beach. You are to come and run along the plank, jump down, come round and do it again. And again. And again."

Spencer Gray and MacCool O'Shea looked at Kell without expression. It was as if he hadn't spoken at all.

"I don't want to play any more games," Cat muttered.

"They won't do it," Bessie whispered. "Look at them. They don't even know enough anymore to come in out of the rain and snow!"

Kell handed her one of the whips. "They will do it right enough," he told her grimly, "for you and I will lay these about their backs until they do as I say."

Bessie Taylor stepped back in shock. "Whip them? Not I! Do you realize what will happen? They will hate us!"

"Hate us?" Kell said fiercely. "Aye, they'll hate us. Pray that they hate us."

"I don't understand . . ."

"I cannot cure the scurvy. But I can give them a reason for wanting to live. Hate. Do you know what hate is? It boils up in the body like a volcanic eruption. It's a passion that sets the blood on fire. It makes the heart beat faster . . ."

"It's evil," Bessie Taylor cried.

"Aye. You'd heal them with love." He nodded ruefully. "A man will die for love. A woman will die for love. But hate . . . there's a witch's brew. A man who hates wants to live, if only for revenge."

"I don't want Cat and MacCool O'Shea to hate me," she said pitifully.

"Their lives are in your hands." Kell would not let her back away from his plan.

Kell asked them, politely enough, to come to the springboard. O'Shea continued to mumble prayers; Spencer Gray muttered to himself in the Maori tongue; Cat hugged Harold, stroking the animal over and over without realizing he was doing so.

The whip in Kell's hand snaked out and caught O'Shea across the back. It crackled again and caught Spencer Gray across his legs. Once again it lashed out; it struck the animal, who ran squealing away in hurt surprise.

"You hit Harold!" Cat jumped to his feet.

"I meant it for you," Kell said evenly.

He drove the two men and Cat before him, herding them toward the beach and the springboard. When they tried to turn aside, they found Bessie Taylor, whip in hand, as merciless as Kell.

"You've got us here," O'Shea said dully. "Are you satisfied then?"

"You're to run along the springboard and jump down." Kell pointed. "It's no more than three feet. Then you'll come around and do it again. All of you, one after the other. Who will be first?"

"The devil take you," O'Shea snapped, beginning to feel anger rise in him. "I'll not play your game."

"I think you will, MacCool." Kell cracked the whip across the small of O'Shea's back. "Move, MacCool! Now!"

Almost weeping with rage, O'Shea climbed to the platform, walked its length, hesitated, then jumped, falling weakly to his knees. Cat came next, then Gray.

"We'd best do the same," Kell told Bessie Taylor. "We need the exercise almost as much as they do."

Without a word, Bessie Taylor walked the plank quickly, leaped down, tripped, rose, and took her place again, the whip steady in her hands.

"Please," Cat moaned after a while, "please, don't make me do it again. I'm so tired."

Kell stood like a man of stone, watching impassively. When he felt they had done enough for this day, he said nothing, merely nodded to them and walked away. Bessie followed him quickly.

"He's a mean, coldhearted man," Cat said. "He's meaner than Rube Gullitt ever was!"

Day after day Kell kept them to the new routine. Walk, jump, go round, climb up. Walk, jump, go round, climb up. Slowly O'Shea and Gray and Cat became less listless.

They came out of their state of despondency, as Kell had predicted to Bessie, boiling with hatred. They threatened him.

"I'll kill you, *pakeha*," Spencer Gray shouted.

"It's the back of my hand to you from this time forward," O'Shea gritted through his teeth at his long-time friend.

"We'll make you sorry," Cat promised.

They plotted against Kell.

"We'll catch him unawares," O'Shea said one day. He was beginning to feel more vigorous again. Each day the exercise became easier, less of a strain. Kell used the whip less and less. Sometimes he just stood silently by, the whip resting quietly by his side.

"The two of us can take him," Gray agreed. "It's time we taught him a lesson."

Cat joined in their secret plan, his green eyes slitted like an aroused tiger.

They jumped Kell the next day, at the springboard.

"No!" Bessie cried. "It's not fair, two against one."

She started forward, but Cat clung to her, hampering her movement.

She struggled to free his grasp, but Cat held on. "I hate him! I hate him!"

"Oh Cat," she said sadly. "He's made you well again. Don't you understand?"

Cat shook his head, brushing her words aside, not wanting to hear what she was telling him.

O'Shea and Gray were grunting with the sheer physical effort of the battle with Kell. They were two against one, but Kell fought vigorously. It was Mac-Cool O'Shea who delivered the blow that felled Kell. He hit the ground and lay there a moment, stunned. Then he sat up, shaking his head to clear it.

"You've a powerful fist, MacCool," Kell said finally. "I was afraid you'd forgotten how to use it."

"He's saved your lives," Bessie Taylor shouted at them. "Can't you see what he's done? Look at you. Could you have raised your hands against him last month, last week? He's put the iron back in your souls."

Now at last Cat understood.

"You wanted us to be mad," he said slowly. "You set out to make us hate you. The exercising every day, the whippings . . ." Cat flushed. "I'll never let anybody ever whip me again," Cat said slowly. "Never."

Kell rose to his feet, rubbing his lip where blood had begun to trickle slowly.

"The whip was a poor weapon," he looked from one to the other in turn, "but it was all I had. I didn't know how else to get you moving again."

"We owe you our lives . . . again," Spencer Gray said, his voice shaking. "But I think, after this, that we will have to make the quarterboat seaworthy and plan to find our way back to New Zealand somehow. I think you know . . . we all know now . . . that life on this island can never be the same."

"He speaks the plain truth, Johnnie," O'Shea agreed. "I think if we do not leave the island, we shall surely die."

17

"Haere Mai — Welcome, My Brothers!"

KELL HAD PROMISED that they would work on the quarterboat and he kept his word. But the daily routine of living went on as well — hunting, fishing, and standing guard on the hilltop.

It was Cat's day to go up to the *mai-mai* and search the sea for sign of a ship. For though they were resigned to the fact that the only way they would leave the island was as Chance, Gullitt, Billy, and Slush had left it, sailing off with hope in the quarterboat, Kell still insisted upon the watch.

Having finished breakfast, Cat walked slowly to the hilltop, with Harold tripping after him eagerly. When he got there, he checked the pile of bracken. The wind had torn at the pile, scattering the branches willfully. Cat began to gather them together again, transferring them to the original heap.

Straightening his back and flexing his shoulder blades — Cat still, like the others, tired easily — his eyes turned automatically seaward. His heart began to thud, a quick erratic beating that made his throat throb. He tried to swallow and could not. On that vast empty sea, one small ship moved, its sails white against the grayness of water and sky.

Cat turned and raced down the hill, tripping in his rush to get back to the camp. He burst in upon the campsite, where Kell, Gray, O'Shea, and Bessie were working steadily on sealskins, preparing them for sails for the quarterboat.

"Sail ho!" Cat shouted as he approached. His voice was delirious with joy. "A sail! To the east! There's a ship to the east!"

"Quick!" Kell called. "Bring torches! We must light the bonfire!"

They picked up torches, which had been prepared long ago against this day, lit them in the fire, and tumbled after one another to the hilltop.

At the lookout, they put their torches to the wood-pile. It burned, but the strong wind kept the smoke from rising, twisting the smoke along the ground, an

earthbound fog of smoke pinned mercilessly down.
Still the ship came steadily on.

"They've got to see us," Bessie cried out. "The ship is heading straight toward us."

The castaways stood riveted, their hopes riding on that lone ship. Kell seemed not to breathe, a giant statue of concentration, willing the ship to come to the island. O'Shea was rubbing his hands, twisting them nervously. Spencer Gray laughed, shouting *"Haere mai* — welcome! welcome!"

"Haere mai!" Cat echoed.

Gray added more branches to the bonfire, then poked at it, stirring the flames higher, hoping to see the smoke spiral upward. But the smoke continued to eddy along the ground.

"Leave off," Kell said suddenly, "or you'll be setting fire to the whole island. She doesn't see us."

Even as he spoke, the ship's sails began to pass from their view, hidden by a bend in the land.

"It's not too late," Cat said urgently. "We can get into the boat and catch the ship near Port Ross."

"She'll be long gone before we ever get there," Kell said. "We must damp the fire, or else the whole island may burn."

"Let it burn, and us with it," O'Shea said, his shoulders sagging with despair. "Better we had never seen the ship at all." He began to move off, back down the path that was well worn after all this time. One by one, the others followed in absolute silence.

At the campsite, they separated, as if they could not bear the sight of one another. Once again, just as they

had before Kell had forced them to run the springboard, they sat or lay about idly, indifferent and without spirit.

When they gathered silently for the evening meal —
driven by hunger — Kell told them of the decision he
had come to during that long day. "We will leave the
island as soon as we have provisioned the boat. She is
as ready as she ever will be. We will sail with all our
skill and faith to guide us. I can offer you no more."

Kell, who had risen to his feet to make his statement,
now left them abruptly. He did not wish to hear their
comments.

Later, the other four castaways sought him out.

"We had a meeting, after you left us," Gray told
Kell. "We have agreed. Better to die at sea, trying to
get back, than to spend any more time here. We will
work as quickly as we can, no matter how weary we
may be, and we will do it willingly." He cleared his
throat nervously. "We want you to know that we are
grateful to you, for everything you have done and tried
to do for us. I would — we all would — like to shake
your hand, John Kell." He held his hand out gravely,
and as gravely Kell took it. O'Shea and then Bessie
stepped forward and took Kell's hand. Cat was last.

"If we live, I'd like to be a man like you someday,"
Cat said simply.

"You're a man now, Cat," Kell answered, his voice
husky with emotion. "You've been shaped in a crucible, laddie."

Now that the decision was hard and fast, they went
about their assigned tasks with determination.

Whatever the future held, Cat thought, if they should

disappear as had Gullitt, Billy, Mr. Chance, and Slush, so be it. Had not all the others on the *Moonraker* been claimed by the sea? Perhaps they were all still bound, in some mysterious way, to that ill-omened ship. Perhaps the sea was calling them, to claim those who had escaped it when the square-rigger died in the cavern.

They worked doggedly all day, Kell and Gray on the quarterboat, going over her inch by inch, Cat searching for birds' eggs to be boiled and stored on the boat, Bessie preparing baked seal, O'Shea hunting for rabbits.

Like the first boat on which Chance and the others had left the island, the second quarterboat had a forward bulkhead built on it, crudely constructed of timber and covered with sealskins. Kell and Gray checked the bulkhead, examined the skins, and studied the mast and the sails.

"We can start putting some of the provisions aboard her tomorrow," Kell said. They all nodded agreement.

The next day, however, a heavy and unexpected hailstorm drove the castaways indoors. Only Cat was abroad. It was his turn to cut wood for the fire. He wielded his ax, stroke by careful stroke. Suddenly he stopped.

"Who's there?" he said, startled. Surely he had heard a voice? A woman's voice? He glanced toward the hut, but the door was closed. Then it was not Bessie Taylor's voice he had heard. He swung his ax up again, poised to strike. Again he thought he heard the voice.

"*Paddy. Paddy, love. Where are you?*"

A tingle shivered up from the base of Cat's spine; a cold shuddering tingle that made him drop the ax.

"Who's there?" he whispered.

"Tell Paddy to go down to the beach. The ship has come."

It's all in my mind, Cat told himself, but the coldness lingered in his spine. It's because Mr. O'Shea was talking about his mother and that long-ago dream he once had. The way he talked about it made it seem real, that's all, Cat comforted himself. That talk and the terrible stillness around me, just the sound of the hail bouncing on the ground, and the ringing of the ax on the wood made me think someone spoke.

"Tell Paddy. The beach. Hurry. The beach."

The voice faded. Petrified with fright, Cat dropped his ax and fled to the hut. He burst in upon the others, white and shaking, hardly able to stammer out a description of what he had just experienced.

"You were daydreaming, Cat," Bessie said kindly. She studied him closely, afraid that he was becoming ill again.

"I know what I heard," Cat said. He shivered. The cold feeling the voice had given him . . . would he ever be warm again?

"Listen!" Gray said suddenly. "The hail has stopped."

"I'm going down to the beach," O'Shea insisted.

"I'm going with you," Cat told him.

One by one they left the hut and headed for the beach.

"The saints preserve you, my darling dear," O'Shea lifted his head and shouted skyward.

A ship rode the water purposefully, close in to the coast.

"To the boat," Kell cried. "We've got to get within hailing distance of her."

"Thank God she came in on the easterly coast," O'Shea muttered. "If she had come in on the west, like the *Moonraker*, she might have been wrecked."

"Her captain must know these waters," Kell agreed. "She's safe enough here, away from those devilish cliffs and the wild seas on the other side of the island."

Kell, O'Shea, and Gray rowed toward the ship, desperation giving them the strength to send the boat racing through the choppy sea. As they neared the ship, they could make out her name — the *Pilgrim*.

On the beach, Cat and Bessie Taylor watched their progress with anxious eyes.

"Ahoy the *Pilgrim*," Kell shouted when they were near enough to be heard.

On board the ship, the captain and his crew stared down at the quarterboat and her occupants, and then glanced toward the beach, where Cat and Bessie had begun dancing in wild abandon.

Captain Harmon, normally a cheery little man, turned to his first mate and said, "What do you make of them, Mr. Chester? They look mad."

The first mate stared at the wild-looking men in the boat, beards and hair long and straggling, dressed in shaggy skins and oddly-shaped conical fur hats, gibbering from the boat, so excited they could hardly be understood.

"Shall we take them aboard?" the first mate asked doubtfully.

Just then Gray spied four Maori seamen, peering

down at the quarterboat from the deck of the ship.

"*Haere mai, haere mai.* Welcome, my brothers," he called.

"One of you can come aboard and speak for the others," Captain Harmon said finally. He waited as John Kell was helped aboard, regarding him suspiciously. Captain Harmon had seen pirates and mutineers in his time. Rescue ships had been taken over by such men and their captains, and crews savaged and murdered. Certainly the captain had not seen a wilder, more menacing appearing lot in a long while.

"Captain," Kell said, as if he could read the other's mind. "You're thinking you've run into a mare's nest of trouble. It's no trap we've set for you. We're survivors of the *Moonraker* . . ."

"The *Moonraker!*" The captain turned to his first mate. "Fetch the craft, Mr. Chester." As the mate went to do his bidding, the captain continued, "We're a whaling ship, out of New Zealand. We had passed the Snares, and some of the crew were fishing. Ah, here it is," he said, as the mate returned. "Caught this in their net." He held up one of the tiny boats with its call for help punched out on the zinc sail. Kell could have wept for joy at the sight of it.

"We ran close round to make the east entrance of Carnley Harbour." The captain chatted on, giving Kell a chance to pull himself together. This wild-looking man, strong as a bear, a bit on the lean side but burly, had tears in his eyes, though his voice was under control now. "The tide was running out and we couldn't enter, so we wore the ship round and stood to the northward, looking for an anchorage on the east side.

We'd have found you," the captain said confidently. "We were planning to search the island for you."

Kell held out his hand for the rough-hewn ship with its plea for help.

"I'd like to have this back, captain, if you'd not be offended by the asking."

"Keep it, man, keep it. You made it after all."

Turning the boat in his hands, Kell said, "If you had not come, captain, we were going to set sail in our quarterboat in a few days, hoping to reach New Zealand."

The captain's mouth fell open.

"You would have sailed across nearly three hundred miles of sea in *that?*" When Kell nodded, he shook his head, began to make a comment, changed his mind and said, instead, "You'll want time to get your things together. We'll come ashore tomorrow and lend you a hand."

Kell clambered down and the three men rowed back to the beach. After the brief hailstorm, ragged spears of sunshine now struggled to pierce the heavy clouds. On the beach, the castaways watched with grateful hearts as the *Pilgrim* anchored offshore.

"What will we do with the quarterboat?" Gray asked practically.

"There may be others who will find themselves lost on these islands," Kell said slowly. "I would wish to leave them better equipped than we were. We'll secure the boat, shelter it. We'll leave sealskins in the huts, along with the tools we've made, whatever will be useful that we don't need for ourselves."

Cat ran his hand over the cards and the dominoes. How hard Mr. Willis had worked over them. Cat could see him now, bending over the tin he had taken from the breadbox, scratching numbers on the tin with a nail. How proud Mr. Willis had been. "I won't leave the cards or the dominoes," Cat said, his eyes bright with tears.

"No," Kell told Cat gently. "You must take them with you when we leave."

They were going to leave the island at last. It was the moment they had prayed for, had fought to stay alive for. Then why, now, was there this feeling of sadness washing over him, Cat wondered.

Like the others, he walked around the island, looking, touching, remembering. There was the hut, with its door standing open now and inside Bessie Taylor, holding the lamp Kell had made, was crying and laughing. Cat backed away. He walked to the frames they had used for drying the sealskins. The frames were empty. Cat ran his fingers along the wood. There would be no more killing, he told himself with fierce joy. Seals could come and sun themselves upon the rocks again in peace. The island would belong to them once more . . . to them, and to the birds. Even the limpets would be safe now.

Cat wandered along the paths that crisscrossed, those well-worn paths over which they had walked each day as they had gone about their tasks of getting food and water. He came back to the pigsties. No need to keep the pigs anymore. Slowly he opened the gate. Surprised, the pigs looked up and then trotted out. It would not take them long to return to their wild state. Harold watched the pigs running off. He trotted after them, but then returned to Cat. Cat flung his arms around

Harold and burst into tears. "You're just a dumb pig, do you know that?" he sobbed, clutching the animal to him. After a while, he stood up and shouted, "Go on, Harold. Go after them. Go on!"

The animal seemed uncertain. He squealed, and, coming closer, nudged Cat on the leg. Cat folded his hands and refused to pet the pig. Harold waited a moment, then turned and ran off to join the others.

Cat wandered down to the beach, scuffing at the ground as he walked, his head down. He was not surprised to find Kell and O'Shea standing and talking at the springboard. They stopped talking as Cat approached. On impulse, Cat ran along the springboard and jumped down to the ground.

"I thought I would hate you forever," Cat said. Then seeing the look of pain that flashed across Kell's face, he added, "I'm sorry, Mr. Kell. I feel all mixed up. I guess we all do, in a way. I know Mrs. Taylor does. She was in the hut, crying and laughing."

Kell and O'Shea looked at each other. O'Shea flung his arms around Kell. "There will never be another like you, Johnnie. I spoke harsh words to you here, on this spot."

"Thank God you were here to speak them," Kell answered lightly. Returning O'Shea's hug, he said, "I think you'd best see to Mrs. Taylor."

"Will you not help me make our last supper on the island, Cat?" Kell asked.

"I think," Gray said from behind them, "that this is one meal we should all make together."

"Do you feel it then, too?" Kell asked gravely. Gray nodded.

It was a quiet meal and a tranquil one. In the harbor, the *Pilgrim* waited at anchor for the survivors.

"Do you think we will ever see each other again, after we get back to New Zealand?" Cat asked.

"I think it's not likely," Kell answered soberly. "We'll be setting our feet on different paths from now on, don't you see, laddie. But what has happened here to us, what we have shared, will always set us apart, all of our lives. We'll not one of us ever be the same again."

"You told me once I'd been shaped in a crucible, here on the island," Cat said, in a low voice. "I wasn't sure what you meant. But I know now . . . I think I can face almost anything after this." He pulled the greenstone jade from beneath his clothing. Turning to Spencer Gray, he said, "You told me, a long time ago, that no harm could come to the wearer of the greenstone jade." Cat glanced toward the *Pilgrim*, riding serenely close to shore. "Whenever I look at the jade, I'll remember you, Mr. Gray, and all the things you told me. And I'll remember Chief E Kehu, too." He slipped the jade back inside his clothing, so he could feel it, resting warmly and comfortingly against his chest.

Cat knew that he would never part with the jade and that he would wear it always, this sacred stone of the Maoris, given to him in friendship. But the gift of life, he realized now, lay not in a symbol, but in the determination and will to survive. He had learned from both men lessons he would never forget.

Next morning, the castaways assembled with their

belongings, ready to walk down to the beach where the crew of the *Pilgrim* waited patiently for them.

"Is it to end like this?" Mrs. Taylor asked suddenly. "Will we not keep in touch with one another?"

Gray leaned over and kissed her gently on the cheek. "We may not see each other again, but we will write." He put his arm around Cat, smiling down at him. "Certainly we will all want to know about Cat."

"I'll write," Cat promised. "I'll write to all of you."

"The time for lingering is over," Kell reminded them.

"Aye," O'Shea agreed.

But at the beach, the castaways stopped and looked back, as if to fix the island and what had happened here forever in their memories.

Kell's words echoed in Cat's mind. *"We'll not one of us ever be the same again."*

Turning away, he joined the others as they stepped aboard the *Pilgrim*, on the first step of the journey home.

Afterword

The Curse of the Moonraker is an historical novel because it is based on an actual event, the wreck of an American-owned vessel, the *General Grant*, an ill-fated square-rigger that left Australia in May, 1866, her destination London via Cape Horn, and carrying among her eighty-three passengers and crew miners who had struck it rich in the Australian goldfields; thus, as part of her cargo, she carried a fortune in gold bullion, nuggets, and gold dust.

Shipwrecks were not an uncommon occurrence in those years. What made this particular shipwreck memorable were the circumstances of the ship's demise — a huge sea cavern in which the *General Grant* foundered, sank, and was entombed — and the fact that of the eighty-three people aboard, fifteen survived, one of them a woman. A battle for survival began for these fifteen on an isolated, uninhabited group of islands of volcanic origin, located in the southern Pacific Ocean, approximately two hundred and ninety miles south of New Zealand. The island group consists of one large and several smaller islands. The large island is called Auckland; one of the smaller islands, to which the castaways eventually moved, was Enderby Island.

The castaways, under the most appalling conditions, survived on the Aucklands for more than a year and a half, primarily because of the efforts of one man among them, an Irishman named Teer, whose ingenuity and determination gave them the gift of their lives. Four of the men, in a desperate attempt to seek help, set off in a quarterboat, without chart or compass, and were never heard of again. A plaque was erected on the Auckland Islands to commemorate the courage and spirit of these four men. Another castaway, a seaman, died on the island. When the castaways were finally rescued, only ten remained.

Many of the incidents described in *The Curse of the*

Moonraker actually occurred; in fact, some of the events that took place have been omitted because, while they were true, they would have appeared to be situations contrived by the author and therefore unbelievable.

One of the tiny craft appealing for help which James Teer, the model for John Kell in the book, made was eventually put on display in a shop in Invercargill in New Zealand and subsequently found a safe niche in the Invercargill Southland Museum. The sealskin clothing of the survivors was also put on display.

The survivors, having lived a life of unbelievable hardship on the Aucklands for eighteen months, were not, upon being rescued, immediately taken to safe harbor, but spent the next six weeks aboard the rescue vessel, which continued on its original sealing expedition.

On their return, the survivors were greeted by cheering crowds. Their story became one of the legends in sea lore. It was kept alive through the years because of subsequent persistent attempts to find the cavern and the supposed fortune in gold entombed there, a search that resulted in additional loss of lives, until the government of New Zealand officially made it illegal to attempt to find the doomed *General Grant*.

Although *The Curse of the Moonraker* stems from these historical facts, it is, however, a work of fiction. Because of this, fictional names are used, and characterizations and the sequence of certain events have been freely altered or invented. There was, for example, no boy among the survivors, and no half-English, half-Maori seaman. In the writing of this book, what had happened has been inextricably interwoven with what never occurred, or, conceivably, might have occurred.

For those who like their history undiluted, and the facts, insofar as they are available, strictly adhered to, this author recommends *The Wreck of the "General Grant,"* by Keith Eunson, a thoroughly researched and well-written work, published in 1974, and highly recommended by the Curator of Colonial History of the National Museum of New Zealand.

The author wishes to express her grateful thanks to the La Trobe Library, State Library of Victoria, Melbourne, Australia, and particularly to Ms. Patricia Reynolds, La Trobe Librarian, for her invaluable aid in supplying source material, to Ms. Janet Horncy, Acting Reference Librarian of the Alexander Turnbull Library, Wellington, New Zealand, to Mr. W. D. Richardson, University Librarian, Baillieu Library, University of Melbourne, and to the Library Council of Victoria, State Library Division, Melbourne, Australia, for their unflagging courtesy and assistance in tracking down source material.

Glossary

The words listed below give only an approximation of the Maori pronunciation in English equivalents. The five vowels in the Maori tongue have both short and long sounds; however, to keep the pronunciation simple, only one form is used here. Accents generally fall on the first or second syllables.

Pronunciation Key

a ma	**i** green	**u** boot	**ai** trying	**ea** air
e hay	**o** dawn	**ae** might	**ao** now	**ou** no

Aotearoa (ow-tair-aw-ah) the land of the long white cloud; New Zealand, with particular reference to the North Island

Ao (ow) light, as the light shining on the surface of water

E Kehu (ay kay-hoo) the chief living on the island

Epikiwati (ay-pee-kee-wah-tee) the Maori name for Spencer Gray.

haere mai (high-ray my-ih) come here (welcome), a favored expression for welcome

Hawaiki (hah-why-kee) the legendary land of the ancestors of the Maoris

Kai-Alua (ky ah-loo-ah) the Maori god of vengeance

mai-mai (my-my) an open-faced rough shelter, closed in on three sides, generally constructed from brushwood and thatched with grass

Maori (mow-ree) native (in the Maori tongue); a Polynesian people who live in New Zealand

Maui (ma-oo-ee) The Maori god who fished New Zealand up from the sea, who harnessed the sun, and who, among other things, is credited with stealing fire from the guardian of the underworld to give it to his people

pa (pa) a protected and fortified village

pakeha (pah-kee-hah) a white person

pohutukawa (paw-hoo-too-kah-wah) a tree in New Zealand, characterized by silvery leaves and scarlet or crimson blossoms; also sometimes called the Christmas tree

pounamu (po-nah-moo) a highly prized stone, used for a variety of tools, weapons, and ornaments; a pounamu was often a symbol of authority

po (paw) blackness; the underworld

rangatira (rahn-gah-tee-rah) a person of high rank; a chief

Tawhiao (tah-whee-ow) a Maori king who led his people in a battle against English soldiers in New Zealand

tapu (tah-poo) forbidden; also sacred

A Selected Bibliography

Armstrong, H. *In Search of Lost Sailors, The Leisure Hour* 1889, pp. 379–385, 463–467.

Bateson, Henry. "The Tragic Auckland Islands," *Sea, Land and Air* 4, 38 (May 1, 1921).

Bridges, T. C. *Heroes of Forgotten Adventure.* London: Harrap, 1938, Ch. 12, pp. 169–182.

Eden, A. W. *Islands of Despair.* London: Andrew Melrose, 1955, pp. 132–142.

Eunson, Keith. *The Wreck of the "General Grant."* Wellington, New Zealand: Reed and Reed, 1974.

Grey, Sir George. "Polynesian Mythology," *A Book of New Zealand,* edited by J. C. Reid. Glasgow and London; Auckland, New Zealand: Collins, 1964.

Harrington, Lyn. *Australia and New Zealand: Pacific Community.* S. Nashville, Tenn: Nelson, 1969.

Kaula, Edna Mason. *The Land and People of New Zealand.* Philadelphia: J. B. Lippincott, 1964.

Lomax, Allen, and Lomax, John. *American Ballads and Folk Songs.* New York: Macmillan, 1934.

McLaren, Fergus. *The Auckland Islands.* Wellington, New Zealand: Reed, 1948.

McLaren, Jack. *My Crowded Solitude.* New York: McBride & Co., 1926.

Maori People, New Zealand Fact Sheet (7), Wellington, New Zealand: New Zealand Information Service.

Rogers, Stanley. *Sea-Lore.* New York: Crowell, no copyright.

Sanguilly, H. D. "Shipwreck of the *General Grant,*" *Harper's Magazine* 38 (March 1869).

Shadbolt, Maurice. "New Zealand, Gift of the Sea," *National Geographic* (April 1962), pp. 456–511.

——. *Isle of the South Pacific.* Washington, D.C.: National Geographic Society, 1968.

Shewan, Andrew. *Great Days of Sail, Some Reminiscences of a Tea-Clipper Captain,* edited by Rex Clements. Boston: Houghton Mifflin Co., 1927.

Smith, C. Harold. *Rahwedia, A True Romance of the South Seas.* New York: D. Appleton and Co., 1927.

Teer, James. "The Loss of the 'General Grant': Narrative of a Survivor." *Wellington Independent,* January 25, 1868.

——. *The Wreck of the "General Grant"* . . . *and the incredible story of James Teer's Gold Watch.* Northern Ireland: Newcastle, Mourne Observer Press, 1962, pp. 1–33.

Watson, James H. "Personal Recollections of Melbourne in the 'Sixties,' " *Victorian Historical Magazine,* 12 (June 1928), excerpt, p. 210.

Wilkins, Harold T. *Gold bugs of Asia and Australasia.* London: Philip Atlan, 1934, pp. 207–212.

The Age, Melbourne, Thursday, March 15, 1866; May 4, 1866.

The Argus, Melbourne, Thursday, March 15, 1866; Wednesday, April 11, 1866.

article in *Wellington Independent,* January 16, 1868.

Imperial Review, January 1888, pp. 63–65.

Illustrated Sydney News, February 22, 1868.

Encyclopedia of New Zealand, vol. 1, edited by A. H. McLintock and R. E. Owen. Wellington, New Zealand: Government Printing Office, 1966, pp. 823–824.

New Larousse Encyclopedia of Mythology. London: Prometheus/Hamlyn, 1959, 1968.